The Maestro

A
MELANIE KROUPA
BOOK

TIM WYNNE-JONES

The Maestro

Orchard Books
New York

The author would like to thank the Canada Council for its support during the writing of this book.

First American Edition 1996 published by Orchard Books
Originally published in Canada by Groundwood Books in 1995

Orchard Books
95 Madison Avenue
New York, NY 10016

Manufactured in the United States of America
Book design by Chris Hammill Paul

10 9 8 7 6 5 4 3 2 1

The text of this book is set in 13 point Monotype Centaur.

Library of Congress Cataloging-in-Publication Data

Wynne-Jones, Tim.
The maestro : a novel / Tim Wynne-Jones.—1st American ed.
p.   cm.
"A Melanie Kroupa book"—Half t.p.
Summary: Fleeing from his brutal father, fourteen-year-old Burl
arrives at the remote cabin of an eccentric genius who in just one
day changes the young man's life forever.
ISBN 0-531-09544-4.—ISBN 0-531-08894-4 (lib. bdg.)
[1. Runaways—Fiction.   2. Child abuse—Fiction.   3. Fathers and
sons—Fiction.]   I. Title.
PZ7.W993Mae   1996
[Fic]—dc20   96-13454

*This one is for Geoff and Carolee Mason,
with fond memories of Pog.*

PROLOGUE

Suckers Run

ONE DAY BURL CROW followed his father to a place on the river where the old man liked to fish. The spot was a secret. Burl hung way back.

Cal was whistling to himself. It was spring. Along the red dirt road there was new velvet on the sumac, new lace on the wild carrot; and here and there hairy stalks of liverwort poked through last year's dead leaves. Spring looked like it was dressing up to go somewhere.

It was odd for Burl to hear his father whistle. Cal was quiet most often, a sullen kind of quiet like thunder a long way off. Then all of a sudden he could Texas two-step himself into a rage and send things hurtling across the room—a plate of mashed potatoes, a broken shoe, a chair with you in it— whatever came to hand. You had to hold on to your seat when Cal was like that.

< 1 >

The whistling led Burl to believe his father was not in one of those thunderhead moods. It gave him the nerve to go on.

It was a foolish game, trailing a man like Cal. But Burl still recalled a time when his father took him places, showed him things. Those times might be lost, but Burl imagined with all the foolishness of a first-class dreamer that when something was lost, you just had to keep hunting for it.

Cal had teased him about the secret spot. "It's a man-sized hole," he said. "You'd get lost—hook, line, and sinker—in a fishin' hole like that."

He had taken to rubbing Burl's nose in things. "Whose limp minnow is this anyway, Dolly?" Burl's mother, Doloris, knew better than to answer.

The secret place was way downstream on the Skat, deep in the bush, at a bend in the river. The water was fast there, shallow but pockmarked with good cold sinks hard by the bank under trailing willow branches. In those green shadows a brook trout could laze around growing awfully big.

From the clumped and crooked cover of the alder scrub above the clearing, Burl could see that the river was swollen with suckers. The suckers were running up the rapids to spawn. You could have shoveled them out. But Cal had only his rod, and he didn't seem in any hurry to use it. He leaned it up against a beached driftwood log. Crouching on the gravel flats right at the water-licked edge, he lit up a cigarette.

The sun glinted off the water, off the backs of the swarming black fish. A bit of a breeze came along to finger through the bulrushes, as if it were looking for something. Just looking, like Doloris fingering through blouses she couldn't afford at the Woolworth down in Presqueville.

The breeze ruffled Cal's thick head of hair, but it never found its way up to Burl in his uneasy hiding place. The blackflies did. They liked the sweaty company of Burl's face.

He swiped at them, his hands whirling in a frantic sign language to which the pesky flies paid no attention.

The flies didn't much bother Cal out by the water. He'd swat his big ropy neck every once in a while. Cal's hand was fleshy and fast. Burl had felt the back of it enough; the palm of it, too. The knuckles were new to him. It was as if Cal had been saving the knuckles as a surprise for when Burl got old enough.

In the cover of the alder brush the blackflies descended on Burl in a cloud. The swarm drew blood; he felt it warm on his hand. Hunting with his father once when things were different, when he could still get close to the man, Burl had seen a bull moose driven suicidal by blackflies. It had crashed out of the bush and hurled its great heaving body into the muskeg, where it swam out deeper and deeper until only its snout could be seen above the water. Burl felt the urge to run now but an even fiercer urge to stay put. He might outrun the blackflies, but he couldn't hope to outrun Cal. Any more than he could hope to saunter down to the river and say, "Nice place you've got here."

He allowed himself to imagine it all the same. He imagined Cal putting out his cigarette and offering him a stick of Dentyne. He imagined them taking off their shoes and socks and wading in amid the suckers, scooping them out onto the gravel, roe squirting out every which way. "How about we fill ourselves a forty-five-gallon drum with these guys, put 'er up in a tree, and bait ourselves some bear?" He imagined Cal saying that.

Then Burl heard a sound from behind him up on the path. It wasn't his imagination. Someone was coming. Someone whistling the same tune as Cal.

Cal heard it. He turned leisurely and his eyes went right to the sound. He dropped his cigarette on the gravel, put it out

< 3 >

with his steel-plated toe. He took out a stick of Dentyne. Then Burl watched his father's face harden into a frown, as if he'd suddenly caught a whiff of something not quite right. His hunter's eyes perused the hillside until he picked his quarry out of the newly green shrubbery.

"There better not be an idiot kid hiding in those bushes."

He spoke loudly, casting his big voice far enough so that the someone coming heard it, too. The whistling stopped abruptly.

"Burl? That you, boy?"

Burl let the blackflies close around him then, like a veil. In his mouth, his ears, burrowing in his hair, crawling up his nose and into the corners of his eyes. He squeezed his eyes tightly shut. But even a fierce dreamer like Burl could not imagine himself out of this. When he blinked, there was Cal coming, crunching across the gravel in thousand-league boots. And Burl's legs shriveled under him.

"You dumb stump-for-brains," said Cal.

Burl untangled himself, broke from cover—too late, always too late—and Cal was on him as quick as a bear on a spawning sucker.

"When you gonna learn to act your age, boy, and not your shoe size."

Burl covered his face. But before he did, he saw the whistler, a blond-haired woman in jeans and a brown suede jacket with fringes all along the arms. She looked anxiously his way and then ran off.

"Now look what you done," said his father. Burl wasn't sure what that might be, except to get himself into a Cal-sized jam.

But before the first cuff landed, another sound came out of

< 4 >

the hot blue May sky. It was a sound like someone beating the air with a giant hand. Swatting the side of the sky as if it were a great blue, stupid son. It was a sound different enough—unexpected enough—to stop Cal's hand, though he did not release his grip on Burl.

The sound grew nearer, a throbbing that drowned out the whir of dragonflies, the chattering of squirrels, the squawking of blue jays. It was not a train. The CPR line passed this way, but no train had ever saved Burl Crow from a beating.

A helicopter. It appeared over the ridge of spruce trees southeast of where Burl stood in his father's grasp. It was a twin rotor, flying low, carrying something large suspended by a long cable.

The boy and the man looked up into the sun as the great noisy chopper approached, a silhouette coming straight for them.

Burl had never seen a grand piano, but he knew that's what was hanging from the cable. Its shadow passed over him before it did. Then for one solitary instant it was suspended above him, blocking out the sun. A black hole in the blue sky. He could see the big bones of its undercarriage, its three solid legs, and a flashing glimmer of its varnished, curvy side.

"Don't you tell no one about this," shouted his father. "Ya hear?"

Burl's head shook violently—he heard, all right—but his eyes never left the chopper. Where had he seen something like this? Not a piano but something else large and helpless. On the TV at Granny Robichaud's. A flood; cattle being airlifted to safety, dumb with shock, leather straps around their fat bellies. The piano was like that, Burl thought—a dumb three-legged animal.

But not dumb. It spoke to him. At the moment it was above

< 5 >

him, even through the shattered air, he heard its song. The wind was playing that thing.

Burl followed the passage of the chopper and its strange cargo north by northwest until it was out of sight. And when he looked down again—his neck aching, dizzy from the sun, dizzy from the vision—his father was gone.

< 6 >

PART ONE

The Good Secret-Keeper

BURL TOOK THAT INCIDENT at Cal's fishing hole, wrapped it in a cloth of silence, and placed it in a small drawer in his thoughts. He didn't want the memory loose in his skull, where it might tumble out of his mouth at the wrong moment.

There were parts to the memory, like the beads on Granny Robichaud's rosary. He remembered her fingering the rosary as she said her prayers. There were small beads and large beads, all held together on a string to help her keep track of the many prayers she seemed to have to say.

On Burl's imaginary rosary there were also many beads: the suckers, the mystery blond, the look in his father's eye. Something more than anger. Maybe even fear.

But the grandest bead of all was the piano. Burl fingered that bead more than any other. It was a warm, smooth black nugget in his mind.

< 7 >

* * *

By the time he was fourteen, Burl was almost as tall as Cal but without Cal's coiled mass of shoulder and gut, and without Cal's ax-handle wrists. Burl next to Cal was like a sapling birch in winter.

Fourteen.

Cal said he must be counting in fairy years. "This boy ain't a day over six, Dolly," he said. Dolly wasn't listening; by then she was all listened out. For his part, Burl curled his shoulders in and stooped low. He made himself small. And he made sure never to stand close enough for the man to notice he was growing up. Burl kept his size a secret.

Burl was a good secret-keeper. If at night he lay awake listening to a train heading somewhere, and if his mind rushed along the track with that train, imagining himself going somewhere, too, he kept the secret to himself. You could shake him up and down the next morning and no train would fall out. What train?

It was the same at school. Knowledge was a thing to keep well hidden. Something to make sure Cal never found on you. He'd want it for sure, and he wouldn't think twice about taking it.

So Burl hid his knowledge away where it might be safe. He built walls around it. Stories.

"What'd you learn at your school today, boy?"

"We learned about the war in Quasiland."

"Where in hell is Quasiland?"

"In Africa. There's a war there."

There was no Quasiland. No war. It was imaginary. If Burl had to—if he was cornered—he could scare up a story in the twinkling of an eye. It saved the truth from getting trampled on by his father. What Cal didn't know, he couldn't hurt.

Burl didn't make stuff up at school. His imagination was

< 8 >

something between him and Cal. But then Mrs. Natalie Agnew came along. She was grade eight, Burl's last year at Presqueville Elementary. She was new in town and hadn't heard about how Burl kept things to himself. Early in the year she got him in after school for a chat.

"I'll write the test again," he said. "Right now, if you want." He stood there, slumping, his arms crossed on his narrow chest. "I know the stuff."

Finally she spoke. "Tell me something I don't already know."

"About what?"

She laughed. "If I knew that, then it wouldn't be something I don't already know."

Burl was on guard. Her face was kind—as far as he could tell—but he wasn't any expert on kindness. Kindness might be a trap. He shut down, waited some more.

"Listen," she said. "Let's talk."

"Then what?"

Mrs. Agnew looked puzzled.

"After I tell you something you don't already know, then what?"

She thought for a moment. "Well, then maybe I'll tell you something you don't know and you'll tell me something else and we'll end up having a conversation."

Burl looked out the window. "Why?" he asked.

They didn't have a conversation that day. So she called him in again. This time she told him it *was* a test. And if he failed it, she'd keep him after school every day until he got it right.

So he thought a bit. And then he told her about his mother's country-and-western band. He told her that his mother was the singer and that the band was called Dolly and the Swing Set, and that she wasn't home often, but when she was it was

< 9 >

a lot of fun. It was all a lie. Mrs. Natalie Agnew had cornered him.

Then she told him a little about herself. About moving north with her husband and building a house together. She went on a bit and then stopped. "I always wished I could sing," she said. "You must be very proud."

There was a long silence. It was painful for Burl. Mrs. Agnew had shiny hair. She smelled pretty. He liked sitting by her desk while she cleared up her papers. But he hated this conversation thing. Hated it.

She must have known. She got up and walked over to a shelf where she kept some books that the students were allowed to borrow. She chose one and handed it to Burl.

"I've got a map I have to draw," she said. "How about you pick a story in here and read to me while I work?"

Burl looked at the cover. *The Red Fairy Book.*

"Out loud?" he asked. Was she serious? She seemed to be. He looked at the table of contents. "Koschei the Deathless," he read.

She didn't look up. She was tracing the outline of the Great Lakes, twirling the pencil point to keep it sharp. "Now that sounds really scary," she said.

"It sounds like my father," said Burl.

There was a bus from the high school in Vaillancourt that passed through Presqueville at five on its way to Pharaoh. Mrs. Agnew arranged things so Burl could catch it on those days when he stayed after class.

Sometimes she would get him to read to her, or she would read to him while he did some classroom chore. And now and then they would have a conversation. Burl would try to think of something worth talking about.

Some of the things he told her were true.

< 1 0 >

He told her about Laura, his sister who had died.

He told her about the dugout canoe his father had made him when he was little.

Then one sunny Monday morning in May, Burl came to school in a state of rare agitation. The others might not have noticed it, but Mrs. Agnew did. His face glowed. His eyes were brimming over with some extraordinary news.

"What is it?" she said. "What are you hiding from me?"

But he didn't dare tell her. Not even about the piano. He couldn't tear the incident at the secret place into separate parts. It was like a rosary. He couldn't show her some of the beads and not others. So he kept it all to himself.

And then school was over and so were his meetings with Mrs. Agnew. She was going to be back south all summer long, but asked him if he would come and visit her in the fall. He said he would.

She gave him *The Red Fairy Book*. He thanked her, but when she wasn't looking, he left it behind in his desk. He was afraid of what Cal might do if he took it home. The only stories that were safe were the ones in his head, wrapped in silence, where Cal couldn't find them.

< 1 1 >

The Antique Lure

SUMMER COMES to the north like a radiant visitor, a fair-weather friend liable to leave in the middle of the night without warning. There weren't many visitors to Pharaoh. Certainly no one came to the Crow house. Cal Crow valued his privacy. But summer came there just the same, even if she never unpacked her bags.

The house was built of scraps of timber, graying chipboard, and peeling tar paper—stuff that Cal had begged, borrowed, or, more likely, stolen. He had built his shack far from prying eyes, up a rutted, overgrown trail that scraped the bottom of his old Plymouth. Burl called the Plymouth the Turd-mobile. But he only called it that out loud once.

Pharaoh, such as it was—a few houses along the rail line, a diner, and a garage with one pump—was not within wailing distance of the Crow place. It was a town of a hundred or so

< 1 2 >

railway workers and foresters and mill hands on a dirt road built to service the CPR track. It was twenty minutes by car down that dirt road to Presqueville, where there were shops Burl's mother couldn't afford to shop in and where Burl had gone to school up until now. In the fall he would be bused to Vaillancourt, another half hour away.

There were a handful of kids his own age in town, a bunch more at the reservation over by Leather Belt, but no one that Burl knew well enough to visit, despite having lived in Pharaoh or near it all his life.

So he spent most of his fourteenth summer fishing, and he did a lot of his fishing up at his father's secret spot.

Cal had his job back at the mill, and Doloris was almost happy, sometimes. Happy to have a few dollars to rub together. Happy to see Cal off early in the morning and coming home late—drunk, most likely, but too tired to do much damage. Burl and his mother shared this almost-happiness, but they did not talk about it. They snuck around the edges of it, afraid Cal might notice and break it.

Burl's mother had some drugs she got from heaven-knows-where. Her "little helpers," she called them. At first Burl liked the idea of her having some kind of help. Then the little helpers seemed to take over, so that Doloris didn't do anything anymore but just sit looking out the window at the bush, which crept a little closer to the cabin every day.

It was dangerous to go to the secret spot—there was no telling how long Cal would keep his job—but Burl went anyway. He enjoyed the thrill of snitching something off his old man. Granny Robichaud once sent Burl some Easter candies when he was little, and Cal ate them all while Burl hopped around like a dancing dog, trying to grab some of what was his. So he would help himself to his father's secrets. That was all he would ever get from him.

< I 3 >

The fishing was good. So good that Burl was afraid the old man might recognize the catch he brought home.

"This is some fish," he imagined his father saying over dinner. "I swear I've seen this fellah before...."

But his father never did. Cal noticed less and less that summer. He seemed a long way off.

Then one day late in August, all that changed. The day started out well enough: a gorgeous hot morning. A morning this deep into the season could turn to a freak snowstorm in a snap, but the heat just piled up on the day like so many hot bricks. The secret place, cool and shaded, called out to Burl.

There was another reason to go there: a new lure, the Brazen Wiggler. That's what his father called it. Actually it wasn't new at all; it was an antique. Cal brought it home from work, said he'd borrowed it from the locker of his smart-ass saw-boss, who bragged a bit too much about tackle auctions and his fancy collection of antique fishing gear.

The Brazen Wiggler was in a little box that Cal opened at the dinner table the way someone else might open a jewelry box. He made a big deal of dangling the antique lure in front of Doloris's mouth, calling her a bigmouth bass, calling her a ling—"Ain't she a ling, Burl? The ugliest fish you'd ever care to snag." He jiggled it in front of her face, hoping she'd lunge for it, take the bait. Doloris stared straight ahead. Cal brought the lure with its wicked three-pronged hook right up close to her lip. "What a catch," he said. Then, laughing, he put the Brazen Wiggler in his tackle box. He loved sport.

That night Burl dreamed of his mother snagged, hauled in, netted, and dragged up over the gunwale of a boat, unable to breathe the air, her eyes scared as she tried to flip back into the water. When he woke up the next morning, he decided to take the Brazen Wiggler himself, since it was already once stolen. He would catch something big. Then he would polish

< 1 4 >

up that new-old lure and replace it before the old man got home.

Burl's mother looked at him from her chair by the window as he took the lure from his father's tackle box.

"You're a blockhead, Burl Crow," she said.

Burl dropped the lure into its little box and slipped it into his pocket. He made sure she saw him do it.

"Your father's right about you," she said. "You're a friggin' blockhead."

Outside, Burl turned back to see her staring hard at him out the window. He waved good-bye. She just stared. Then he moved on, the light shifted, the window went black, and his mother's face vanished.

One of the marvels of the secret clearing on the Skat was that there was nearly always something of a breeze, even when the way that led there was dusty going and gunmetal hot. On the gravel spit that poked its crooked finger out into the river, Burl cast out his line.

The sun was dazzling, the wind clean on his face and bare arms. He saw a straggly line of geese heading south.

He was reeling in his line, thinking about a swim, when something hit the Wiggler. A trout, but not one he'd seen before: a rainbow. It jumped and slapped back down, dragging him this way and that up and down the gravel shore and out into the stream, where the water cut at his ankles like little razors. A rainbow trout escaped from some hatchery or stocked stream, perhaps, and now his, if he could only reel it in. At last he pulled it up onto the shingle at his feet, where it danced its death dance and shone in the sun, an arm's length of mottled, muscled silver.

He knelt beside it and with his penknife cut the Wiggler

free, for the fish was gut-hooked. And that is when the girl arrived.

She didn't see Burl. At least, he didn't think she did. He was on his knees when something made him look up, and there she was on the bank. Instinctively, he crouched lower. Her eyes did not turn his way. He slithered lower still until the gray bulk of a driftwood log came between them.

It was not the blond in the fringed jacket. This one was the brown-haired girl who worked at the diner in Pharaoh. She was still in her white blouse and short black waitress skirt. She looked out of place. There was no one here to take orders from. She undid her hair. It caught the sun in a coppery flare. She undid the top two buttons of her blouse.

Burl didn't know where to look anymore. The rainbow slapped hopelessly at his knee. He lay down slowly on the gravel beside the dying fish. He placed the Brazen Wiggler back in its box and slipped it into his pocket. He lay his head down on the hot stones.

When he dared to look again, the girl was leaning back on her elbows in the grass. What was her name? His father sometimes sent him to the diner for cigarettes. Burl tried to recall the name tag she wore on her breast. Tanya. That was it. As he watched, Tanya sat up again and took a cigarette from her handbag.

She checked her watch. She smoked. She looked back from time to time up the path, but she never looked his way.

The trout twitched its last. Burl squirmed himself lower into the stone bed like a spawning fish, wishing he could bury himself on this warm shore. Scales glittered on his knife blade. He cleaned it off on his shirttail.

When he looked again, Tanya was sitting up. He watched her find a compact and check her face in the mirror. She fluffed

< I 6 >

out her hair, chucked the compact back in her bag. A sound sifted down to Burl. Someone whistling.

Burl's first instinct was to warn the girl. He was afraid of what might happen if Cal found her in this of all places. Then Cal arrived at the end of the path. He stood with his hands on his hips, looking at her. Burl held his breath. Cal tipped his cap at Tanya and moved in on the bank beside her. She took a cigarette from her bag and, lighting it with her own, placed it between Cal's lips. He took a long drag.

Burl laid his face down hard against the stone shore and fought to breathe, his mouth wide open.

He craned his head to see them. His father was laughing. Burl couldn't hear what they were saying. And now Tanya was holding something out of his father's reach and his father was grabbing for it, but it was all in play.

Something rose in Burl. It was hot like vomit in his throat, but it rose until it filled up his head, straining against his skull.

Cal did not see Burl rise from behind the driftwood. He was still trying to grab whatever it was Tanya was keeping from him. Tanya saw Burl; Cal followed her gaze. He shook his head, swore under his breath, climbed to his feet. Tanya stood up, too, using Cal's arm for support.

That's when the top of Burl's head blew off.

"YOU STEAL EVERYTHING!" he screamed, and he charged across the gravel spit toward them. "EVERY-THING."

His voice fell apart at the seams—nothing but a boy's high-pitched squeal. He slipped and fell and got up again and scrabbled up the hill with his knife out before him like a tiny lance.

"Cal, do something," said Tanya nervously, taking a step behind him. But Cal just threw back his head and laughed.

"This oughta be good," he said.

< 1 7 >

His father waited for him, cocky with someone to impress. He stood in a brawler's wide-legged stance, knees bent, rolling his shoulders, his hands loose.

Burl had only one chance, and it wasn't his pip-squeak knife. He veered suddenly and sharply like a jet fighter peeling out of a tight formation and shot up the path toward the road. By the time Cal regrouped, Burl's legs had put fifty long strides of bush between the two of them.

"You'll pay for this!" Cal shouted.

"Not this time," said Burl. The words were salty with sweat, but they tasted sweet in his mouth. "Not ever."

< 1 8 >

North by Northwest

WHEN BURL WAS FIVE he got lost. They were traveling west to Dryden to visit Granny Robichaud. It was before Laura died. They camped along the way, and at every campsite his father told him and Laura—she was eight—not to wander off.

"If you get lost, find a stump and park your backside on it."

But Burl wandered off. Way off. It took a search party to find him. Cal shook him hard.

"What'd I tell you, boy?" he said. "Why'd ya keep goin'?"

"I was looking for a stump," Burl told him.

You don't need to find a stump if you have no intention of being found. Burl wasn't five anymore. He was fourteen and growing up with every step. By the time he hit the CPR rail

< 1 9 >

bed, he was a little older than he had been back at the secret place. He ran along the rails a way, breathing in hot creosote, putting a thousand railway ties between himself and his father. By the time he hit the service road to Pharaoh, he was older still. And by the time he passed the abandoned hotel, the turn into the mill, the back way to the reservation at Leather Lake, he was really getting on in age. Childhood dripped off him in great huge gobs of sweat.

He turned down a logging trail he knew and finally stopped. His mouth hung open, gulping in air. It was cooling down. The sun was low over the forest. He had a stitch in his side. In the trees he heard a woodpecker.

Burl's best bet out of Pharaoh would have been to hop a freight train. He'd seen a guy do it. The trains slowed down and you ran along and jumped at the ladder. Always the ladder at the front of the car. That way, if you missed, you'd just bounce off the side. If you missed the ladder at the end, you'd fall into the space between the cars. And that was that.

But if you caught that first ladder, you could lie low on the roof and sleep under the stars all the way to White River. At White River you could hop off and hitch a ride up the Trans-Canada. The brother of a kid at school did that once. He broke his ankle when he jumped off, but he still made it all the way to Winnipeg.

Then there was the highway. The new 144 up to Timmins, which crossed the railroad a few miles north of Pharaoh. Or, if you could get down to Presqueville, you could take the 505 out to 17. If you wanted to avoid the police, you had to be flexible. That is, assuming someone was looking for you. Burl wondered how many days his folks would wait for him to come back. They didn't have a phone. And try as he might, Burl couldn't imagine Doloris making it into Pharaoh to alert the authorities.

< 2 0 >

When Laura died, Doloris kept setting a place at the table for her for weeks before the old man hurled the plate against the wall, smashed it to bits. Burl wondered if she would keep setting a place for him.

The truth was, Burl knew all sorts of ways of getting away from Pharaoh. When you lived under the same roof as a man like Cal, you had to be ready to run and hide at a moment's notice. You learned to recognize the signs of a foul mood. The old Turd-mobile arriving in the yard too noisy, the engine revving too high, the car door slamming, footsteps too heavy on the porch. Then you had to be quick. Into the closet— the one Cal never finished—where you could squeeze way back out of sight and out of reach in between the studs of the wall. A place too small for a big man like Cal.

But Burl had grown too big for rabbiting himself away in cubbyholes. So he kept his ears open for bigger hiding places: Winnipeg, Toronto, Dryden. Dryden was big compared to Pharaoh or even Presqueville, but it wasn't big enough. Cal would stomp into a town like Dryden and pluck the roofs off every house until he found Burl.

North by northwest. The bush he knew, at least a bit. He was too busy running away to worry yet about where he was going. And it didn't occur to him, not on that first blood-hammering-in-the-head afternoon, that he was actually heading somewhere.

There are paths in the forest. There are privately owned logging roads and way older overgrown trails from the days when logging was done in winter and horse-drawn sleighs dragged the lumber to the edge of a lake or river. Even older than the sleigh roads are the native portage trails. Then there are trap lines and survey lines. Burl knew something about paths.

And there are signposts: a rocky outcrop the shape of a

< 2 1 >

head; a giant jack pine split by lightning; a burn area, the enormous black thumbprint of a forest fire. Burl knew something about signposts.

Cal was a hunter, and for a while when Burl was younger, the old man had taken him along. By the time he was six, Burl had learned how to clean a rifle and oil up the barrel. He could pluck a mallard or gut a pike or follow blazes cut into trees. Burl remembered playing soldiers with shotgun shells while waiting out a drizzle under a tarp slung between dripping spruce trees. He remembered men joking and smoking. His dad hadn't been so bad in those days, not when he was out in the woods.

But then Cal's fortunes changed. His friends changed. Hunting and fishing expeditions got longer with less game to show for them. And Burl didn't get to go along anymore.

But he had a sense of this part of the wilderness. There were still paths and signs to follow, and beyond that, he had a pretty good store of wilderness knowledge. Cal had given him that much.

"You steal everything!"

Over and over he replayed the scene at the secret place. Sometimes he killed Cal—drilled his little pocketknife right into Cal's heart. Then Tanya, released from her evil spell, would fall at his knees and beg his forgiveness. Sometimes he would forgive her. Sometimes Mrs. Agnew showed up and stood with him over the dead body of his father.

"So this is Koschei the Deathless," she would say.

"Not anymore," Burl would answer.

He imagined going home. He imagined saying brave things and doing brave deeds. But he didn't slow down.

It got dark about nine or so. And just as the shadows were getting thick and the birds were having their mad half hour before the world ended, and just as the mosquitoes came out

<2 2>

looking for blood, Burl came across an old trapper's shack. He hadn't known it would be there, but he took it as a sign. Somebody was looking out for him. That's what he told himself.

Not that it was much of a sign. The door had been torn most of the way off its hinges. Deep gouges in the weathered slabs indicated a bear's work. There was garbage scattered around the cabin's single room and a huge dried-up bear turd sitting prominently in the center of the floor. Weeds grew through the floorboards. Porcupines had eaten away a part of the roof. The forest was reclaiming this place as its own.

But there was a rust-stained mattress on the floor, which was more than he had hoped for. And as far as he could tell, nothing had been living there recently. There were no bowls of porridge cooling on the table.

He found a can without a label. It had rolled into a corner. There were bear-sized tooth marks in it. He pried up the top with his knife blade. Baked beans. He drank the contents cold. He had no matches.

He sat on the mattress, mosquitoes buzzing around his ears. He found himself hoping it would be cold that night so that he might sleep in peace. But then, if it was cold, what peace would he find with no coat, no cover, and only half a roof over his head.

There was a cup sitting on the floor beside the bed. In it was a harmonica. He picked it up, looked it over. He rubbed it as clean as he could with the tails of his shirt. He took a tentative blow. No sound. It was full of dust and pollen. He banged it hard against the palm of his hand. Blew again. The notes came out dry and lifeless. He blew harder into the little chambers from both sides, until finally he was able to clear enough guck out to blow a few good, ringing notes.

Burl pulled his feet up onto the mattress and curled them

< 2 3 >

under him. Leaning his back against the wall, he tried to think of a tune to play, a tune with just a few notes. He closed his eyes.

Rain beat down on the cabin. It moved in with him but was not content to share the space. As the wind gusted, the rain, like a predator, stalked Burl across the mattress, cornering him.

Something gouged him sharply in the thigh. He dug his father's stolen lure from his pocket. One hook had poked through the carton, sweaty and rain-soaked; the barb was caught in the lining of his pocket.

He sat up, shivering with cold, and tried to work the hook out in the darkness. From his other pocket he took out his knife and cut the hook free. Then he rolled himself up as tight as a millipede in a dead log. Someone watching over him? Not likely. He lay his hands protectively over the lure and the knife and the harmonica. They were all his worldly possessions.

It was a night of strange music: the rain banging on the tin roof, something rustling the bushes not far off. An owl, a whippoorwill. Wolves. A piano. No. That was just a dream. But so real-sounding. In Granny's church in Dryden there were angels. Burl wondered if this was what it was like when they played their harps. A cold, thin, distant sound as sweet as blackberries before they're quite ripe.

< 2 4 >

The Lake

WHEN YOU WERE HUNGRY in a fairy tale, an old hag would pass by with a magic bowl or magic beans. Well, Burl had eaten what beans he could find, and when he awoke cold and damp in the morning, sure enough, the can was full again, but only with brown rainwater.

So he took a bite of the north wind for his breakfast and headed out, up a path that had once been a trap line, until it petered out and there was finally nothing before him but bush.

In a fairy tale, the woods might be deep but the paths led to a river where you could trick the boatman; to a castle where you could steal a golden goose; to a clearing in the forest where you could kiss a princess in a glass coffin. Fairy-tale trees towered darkly above lost children, but there was always a way.

Sometime around noon, Burl stumbled upon a small green

<25>

stream heading the same way he was going. He cooled his scratched and bleeding legs in the dark water. No trout in a stream like this, a dead stream. But it widened, and he meant to wade as far out as he could from shore and the leaning wall of vegetation, the better to escape the mosquitoes and blackflies and deerflies. A few steps out, however, his foot sank deep into the mud, and, flailing wildly, he fought his way back to a firm footing. A loon-shit bottom, his father would have called it.

He found blueberries past their prime by the edge of a stagnant pond and ate until he could eat no more but was only hungrier for his effort. The blueberries reminded him of food.

He came to a place where the still stream widened out into a sphagnum bog. Seeing that the farther shore was rockier and less overgrown, he crossed on the spongy mattress of living plants, feeling it give under his every step but never give way.

In the low branches of a tree on the far shore he came upon a deserted robin's nest. There were two abandoned blue eggs.

Burl had never eaten a raw egg before, but he had heard of people doing it, and his hunger nudged his hand forward. He cracked the egg carefully so as not to lose any of the insides. But the minute it was cracked, a hideous rotten smell and a glimpse of wet feathers made him hurl the egg away. He stumbled, gagging and spitting the smell out of his throat.

He found his way along the shore of what turned out to be a massive beaver pond. High granite cliffs rose above him.

He came upon a dried wolf's turd full of red fur.

He came upon saplings draped with the velvet off a moose's antlers.

He came upon a tree used as a scratching pole by a bear.

He marked the sun when he could see it through the clouds.

He crossed the beaver dam, slipping in the rushing water,

< 2 6 >

bruising his knee. There was a way up the cliff here, but even as he started to climb, the rain came on hard, driving down. He cut away from the shore and took shelter in the deeper woods. He stopped in a grove waist-high with Labrador tea. Moose loved this shrub. Once, when his father had shot a moose, he slit its carcass open, and buckets of Labrador tea poured from the beast's belly. When the twigs, leaves, and flowers were young, they were aromatic; natives and trappers made tea from it. But when Burl tasted it now, with summer mostly gone, the fuzzy-bottomed leaves only made him gag.

He recognized a mushroom he thought he'd seen his father eat. He sawed through the stem with his pocketknife, only to find the center eaten away by maggots.

The rain pelted down. Could he go back? His eyes closed; he walked backward in his mind through this long day to the cabin where he had spent the night. From there ... yes ... it was possible. He could make that choice, though it grew less possible the farther he went. But back to what?

Burl hunkered down in the scrub, the rain beating down all around him. In the boggy earth at his feet he saw a fly climb into the inviting purple mouth of a pitcher plant. He watched the fly turn to leave, buzzing furiously as the bristles of the inner cavity made it impossible to get out. It buzzed helplessly. Then, soon enough, it fell into the small pool of water at the base of the pitcher, where it drowned.

How easy to be a plant. You just stayed put and food fell into your lips. His eyes tightly closed, Burl tilted his head upward and let the rain beat on his tongue, drizzle down his throat. He slept in fits and starts. Maybe a lifetime passed while the rain pelted down. In any case, he was a little older when he woke up.

The rain let up. Burl found his way back to the dam and began the ascent of the cliff. The rain had released a heavy

< 2 7 >

perfume of pine and ozone. The sun came out. And so did the mosquitoes, to prey on his raw skin. He was too weak, too busy climbing, to swat at them.

At the top he started to run along the cliff, following the length of the enormous beaver pond. He heard cries, and up ahead in the rinsed-out sky he watched two small birds dive-bombing an osprey. An osprey. Burl was sure of it. And that meant a lake, a true lake with fish in it. He raced along the ridge. Below him the beaver pond was narrowing to a bottleneck, the head of the pond. Across the pond he could see the cliff fall away, and then, suddenly, he broke through a wall of spruce and found himself on the cliff head. A bald promontory that dropped sharply.

And there below was a lake. A high-sided lake of deep, green water with the far edges pale golden with rushes. There was a strong enough breeze on the cliff top to keep the mosquitoes at bay, and so he sat, breathing heavily, drying out a bit. Across the lake stretched low hills of poplar with darker patches of pine like deep green inkblot stains on a gold ground.

In a lake like the one below there would be fish, all right, but Burl was not an osprey, fitted with powerful vision and sharp claws, able to dive for his supper. He had a lure and a harmonica but no rod and no line. Now if it were a magic harmonica, the fish would rise to hear him play and dance on the water right into his hands.

Under the late-afternoon sun he became angry. Angry that these fairy-tale words came unbidden to his mind. Useless ideas.

Then his anger shifted gears. He saw his father again with the cocky smile on his face, waiting for Burl to attack. Cal had won the fight. Surely all he had wanted was for Burl to leave. Then he became angry at Tanya and at his mother, and at Laura for dying and leaving him alone, and that made him

< 2 8 >

angry at himself all over again until he was dizzy with anger. Dizzy with hunger, dizzy with the sun, dizzy with longing.

When he could see clearly again, he noticed there was a small beach at the base of the cliff. Chunks of the cliff had fallen off; great square boulders littered the sandy shore. He began to slither down the rock face on his backside, reaching for toeholds, grabbing at roots and bushes to slow his descent. Halfway down he knew he no longer had any control. He was falling. Gravity was tugging him down at its own relentless speed. And then he was in the air, the rock curving back behind him. The free fall landed him in a heap on the sand.

The sand was hot. The westering sun was falling on this parcel of beach between two boulders taller than he was. He turned; there was a cave he could sleep in. Burl pulled off his sopping shoes and dug his toes into the clean warmth of the sand. Then he squirmed out of his clinging wet clothes, which he hung from a tree that grew from a cleft in the rock. Without a thought to how cold the lake would be, he hurled himself into the water, splashing out until his tired legs could walk no farther, then crumpling happily into the numbing coolness of it. He floated on his back, kicking until he was a good way offshore, where he lay, a dead man floating peacefully with only his face above the glinting surface.

At first he thought that what he was hearing must be some kind of underwater creature, though he knew of no inland fish that could sing as whales or dolphins do. It was music. He treaded water, lifting his head above the surface of the lake, shaking the water from his ears. He was far enough out from the shore to see around the cliff head he had just descended and into a small, gently curving bay.

At the head of the bay was a structure like nothing he had ever seen before, a gray shingled pyramid with tall triangular windows. There was also a broad deck that narrowed to a

< 2 9 >

lower deck. It was from this building—for there were no others on the lake—that the sound must be coming.

It was a piano. And the song glided out to Burl from the pyramid like a small boat on the green lake in the sun-drenched air. He had only to climb aboard, and the song would take him there.

< 3 0 >

Interview with the Baron

BURL SWAM BACK TO SHORE with long hard strokes. He emerged shivering from the lake, the flesh on his arms goose-pimpled. With the sun scarcely rimming the hills, the air was already turning chill. Any night now there would be a frost.

He shimmied into his wet jeans, hating the way they clung to his legs. He couldn't bring himself to put on his shirt. It stank of sweat, and the neck was bloodstained from the attacks of insects. So he set off toward the pyramid house half-naked, carrying his shoes and shirt. And as he rounded the cliff into the bay, he felt as if he were carrying his heart, too, the way you carry a moth from the house to let it go outside, aware of its beating against your hands.

The sandy beach at the cliff head did not stretch all the

< 3 1 >

way to the cabin. Here and there the brush tumbled right to the edge of the lake.

Sometimes Burl lost the music. He couldn't tell if it was because it stopped or only grew quieter or whether it was just a trick of the wind. There were many notes, more notes than Burl could imagine anyone playing. One of his teachers played the national anthem on special occasions. But this music was like ten national anthems played at the same time, as if an anthem were sprouting from every finger. And it went on and on, growing and then mysteriously vanishing.

The huge triangular window reminded him of a sail, and, like a sail, it seemed alive in the breeze, filled one moment with a reflection of water and sky and the next emptied and replaced with geometric blocks of shade. But there was a piano in the window, and a person bent over the keyboard.

Then the music really did come crashing to a halt, seemingly in mid-phrase. The someone in the window sat hunched and still as if in prayer for a long moment and then rose, uncoiling to the length of a man, and moved out of Burl's view.

A half-dead pine stretched out from shore across Burl's path. Wading around it out past his knees in the lake, Burl approached the cabin, hugging his shirt high to his bony chest. His teeth chattered. A screen door opened and slammed shut. A man appeared on the deck and made his way down a short flight of stairs to the lower deck, which nudged out over the water. He leaned on the rail and looked toward where the sun had been only a few minutes earlier but where now there was just the orangy pink glow of its passing.

He was stooped a bit, balding, and dressed in a heavy gray coat, a scarf, and a flat hat. He took a cookie out of a box but paused with it halfway to his mouth, as if struck by a thought. He raised the cookie, held it poised in the air, and then he began to wave it around. Not waving, thought Burl.

< 3 2 >

Conducting. As if he was not on a deck at all but on the podium of a music hall and there was an orchestra below him on the lake. The man was wearing gloves with the fingers cut out of them.

The man was humming, lost in the music. Burl plucked up his courage and waded toward him. The man—cookie baton raised—stopped conducting, stopped humming. He looked toward Burl, fixed him in his gaze. He didn't speak until the boy was standing directly below him.

"Let me guess who you are," he said. His face hovered above Burl. It was haggard, but his eyes were alert and blueberry blue.

"You are, by ze looks of you, a second bassoon player," he said in an imperious voice. "Vell, I'm sorry, you're too late. Ze position has already been filled. Good day."

He dismissed Burl with a wave of his hand. But Burl did not move. "I wonder—"

"No, vait!" said the man. He took another cookie from the box, an Arrowroot cookie, and took a thoughtful bite. "I've got it wrong. You're ze new public relations fellah from Columbia Records—zey get younger every year—und you've got a slate of interviews with ze press lined up for me. *Ja*?"

Burl looked behind him.

"Oh, zey vill be arriving any minute by limo-canoe." The man grabbed the throat of his coat in his fist, and his voice rose in mock panic. "Und you vant me shaven und shorn und looking my best or you'll never be able to sell ze new album."

Burl's attention to this performance was distracted by the box of cookies.

"No, no!" said the man, clicking his fingers. He leaned deeply over the railing to better look into Burl's eyes. "You're a *child*. Am I correct?" He had dropped the German accent.

Burl swallowed hard. "I'm fourteen."

< 3 3 >

"I talked to a child once," the man replied. "He drank a glass of milk while I ate breakfast. Scrambled eggs, I think it was."

Burl looked down. A school of minnows swam around his feet, which were as still and coldly white as rocks. His legs felt numb. He looked up again. The man was looking away, squint-eyed, across the lake. Then, without a glance at his visitor, he turned and walked toward the door. He was leaving. Just like that. Burl panicked.

"Hey!" he said. "Wait."

"You don't appreciate my masquerade," said the man without turning back. He sounded hurt, though Burl felt certain this was all part of the act. Quickly he stuffed his shoes and shirt under his arm and began to clap. He clapped loudly. The minnows at his feet scattered in alarm.

The man returned to his post at the rail. He bowed deeply.

"A standing ovation," he said. "You're too kind."

Burl was almost afraid to stop clapping, afraid that the man might leave again, the show over, the audience forgotten. But when he did stop, the man's face had lost some of the intensity that had overtaken him when he was playing at his guessing game. It was then that his dazzling eyes took note of the object toward which Burl's gaze helplessly drifted. He handed down the box of Arrowroots.

"So it's my victuals you're after, is it?"

"Thank you," said Burl.

The man sat in a deck chair. "Do you plan on standing around in the drink all night?"

With his hand shaking badly, Burl fished a handful of cookies from the box and shoved them into his mouth. He did not move until the Arrowroots had dissolved to sweet gruel. Crumbs fell into the lake and the minnows returned, shooting to the surface to feed.

< 3 4 >

"Well?" called the man impatiently. "Are you about ready to explain your purpose here?"

Burl did not waste any time. He made his way around the lower deck, waded ashore, and climbed a short flight of stairs.

"I had the deck built like one of those observation platforms they have on whalers, but do you think I've seen a single whale? Nothing. *Nada. Nichts.*" The man was stretched out in his chair, his long legs fully extended before him. His overcoat was stained; the hem had come undone. A button was missing, and Burl could see a second, charcoal-colored coat underneath. The man was in stocking feet; one big toe stuck through a hole in a tired gray sock.

"Have a seat," he said. He ran his hand over his unshaven face, through his bedraggled hair. Burl could not take his eyes off the man's fingers. So pale, so long.

He looked around and noticed there wasn't another chair. So he settled himself cross-legged on the deck. The man looked pleased. The tiredness left his face. He looked at Burl in a new way. "I looked like you once," he said. Burl self-consciously pushed his hair back from his face. The man laughed. "Young, I mean. I not only looked young, I *was* young. Hard to believe, isn't it?" He leaned forward on one elbow and made a face. "You are probably vondering vhat ees place und who your distinguished host might be, *ja?*"

"Yeah ... yes," said Burl. "Kind of."

The man looked delighted. He poked Burl in the knee.

"I am none uzzer zan ze famous conductor und Arctic wise guy, Gustav von Liederhosen. *Baron* von Liederhosen to you."

"Oh," said Burl. He wrapped his arms around the box of Arrowroots. "Thank you for the cookies, Baron."

"Are you not astounded beyond your vildest dreams?"

Burl was certainly bewildered and vaguely frightened. But he was also fascinated, and, more important than any of the

< 3 5 >

feelings that raced through his tired brain, he was in need of food and somewhere to stay. Something told him that the baron's performance required a performance in kind.

"There aren't many conductors around here."

"I should say not!" said the baron, smiling smugly.

Burl popped another couple of cookies in his mouth, not certain how long he would have possession of the box or the favor of this changeable character. He looked away.

"Och! You look flustered, my *Wildeskind*."

"I'm kind of lost," said Burl.

"Ah, well, that makes two of us, old chap." The baron's accent had shifted suddenly to that of a British gentleman. "At least I had every *intention* of being lost. But now it seems you've found me out. Bearded me in my lair, as it were, what."

Burl stared at the man. "What happened to the baron?" he asked.

"What a remarkable boyo," said the man. "I have very adeptly adopted—say that quickly, three times—the disguise of Sir Chauncey Cakebread, eminent musicologist and rocketeer."

"Oh," said Burl again. This was hard to keep up with. It was also, somehow, embarrassing. Burl had never been paid so much attention in his life. He was drowning suddenly in attention. He could not look up. He ate another cookie. The pause lengthened. He stole a glance at the man, hoping he hadn't hurt his feelings, wondering if he should have clapped again.

The baron, Sir Chauncey—whoever he was—was staring at Burl, his face in repose again, but puffier, wearier than it had been only a moment earlier. He dug a pair of dark-rimmed glasses from a pocket inside his coat and looked at Burl more closely. Burl was looking toward the window where the grand piano sat.

< 3 6 >

When the man spoke again, his voice was kind and sincere sounding. "What is it, *Wildeskind, enfant sauvage,* wild child?"

Burl cleared his throat. "Your piano," he said. "I saw it before. Last spring. I followed it here."

The man seemed to pierce him with his gaze. "You followed it?"

"Well, not exactly. I saw it flying—I mean, being carried by the helicopter—and I kind of started out in that direction."

The man's eyes grew wide with wonder. Then a mosquito landed on his ear, and he slapped it and grimaced.

"Ah, the joys of twilight in the north." He clambered out of his chair and, ducking his head in his collar, hurried to the door. He turned as he opened it. "Quick," he said conspiratorially, waving Burl toward the door. "Inside, *mein Kind,* before ze rest of his pesky friends discover us, too."

< 3 7 >

Take Two

THE BARON MADE scrambled eggs. He hummed while he cooked and waved the spatula as if he were directing a silent symphony.

The inside of the pyramid was one large room. To Burl— who had grown up under stained and buckled corkboard— it seemed more like a church than a dwelling. But it was not a fancy church, not like Grandma's church with the bleeding Jesus and the stained-glass windows. Only the piano was fancy. It was as long as a boat and as unlikely inside the cabin as a boat might be. A sleek black boat with curving sides.

Nothing else about the cabin looked finished. Roofing nails poked through the sloping ceiling; there were no walls except for a blanket draped across one corner to hide a composter toilet. There was scarcely any furniture to speak of. The kitchen corner consisted of a counter unit with a built-in sink, stove,

< 3 8 >

and mini-fridge, and shelves stocked mostly with canned food. Burl's host occasionally tapped on a can or two with his flying spatula, in rhythm to his hum.

The sink was piled high with unwashed dishes. The place was messy, and yet, oddly, it did not look lived in. The floor was covered in a dull-gray carpeting. There was no bed but only a mattress, the bedclothes rumpled, and several books piled or open beside a bedside lamp. There was an open suitcase from which a jumble of clothes spilled.

There were two tables in the room, with a single chair at each. One table was for eating. The other table was being used as a desk. It was littered with writing paper, notes, and an open book or two. But there were also several neater piles, with a rock paperweight on each. The rocks held down large-sized music sheets on which notes had been scribbled in pencil. There were words scribbled underneath the clefs. There was a cracked black cup full of pencils.

But the room was dominated by the piano. It sat by the window that looked out over the lake. Burl touched its glossy curving side.

"Soup's on," said Burl's host. For all his flair for performance, he flopped the food onto the plate the way one emptied something rotten into the garbage, and then he dropped the pan into the sink hurriedly. The eggs were overcooked, but there must have been several of them, and the scrambled mess looked wonderful to Burl.

"This ought to get you through to dinner," said the man. "Or do you call it supper? I've never been entirely sure which was which."

Burl ate a large steaming mouthful. Too large a mouthful and too hot. He needed water, but his mouth was full, and the cook seemed oblivious to his frantic gestures.

"Well?" asked the man.

< 3 9 >

Burl swallowed at last, gasping for air. "Water."

"Oh, good," said the man, his eyes brightening. "Word associations. I like that. Let's see ... train!"

Burl fanned the air in front of his open mouth. "Train?"

"No, no, no. Something different. I say 'train' and you say 'tunnel' or 'engine' or whatever you like. Whatever comes to mind. Heavens, child, you started the game."

"Started what?"

"When I said 'well,' you said 'water.'"

Burl was puzzled. He looked at his plate. Took another mouthful—hot or not—afraid now that it might be snatched away from him at any moment.

"Harrumph," said the man. "Not a sportive child, I see." But the next thing Burl knew, the fridge was opened and the man was pouring him a glass of Orange Crush, which he placed on the table. "Hot?" he asked.

Burl took the glass and greedily drank from it. He looked over the rim at his host, who eyed him expectantly. Burl lowered the glass.

"Cold," he said.

His host smirked, a triumphant glint in his eye. Then he sighed, stuck his hands into the pockets of his bulky coat, and walked over to the window to look out upon the lake.

Burl ate in silence. He was glad to eat, but he found the silence vaguely disturbing. At home a quiet meal was something to pray for. But this man, who seemed to turn himself on and off as if by a switch, was more interesting when he was talking. More alive. Now he seemed to be brooding. Burl swallowed, wiped his lips with the back of his hand.

"Supper," he said. "At night it's supper."

The man did not turn. "And you call a place like this a camp. Whereas where I come from, we'd call it a cottage."

"It's great," said Burl.

< 40 >

"Ah, well. But the important thing is, is it a great supper?"

"It's real good," said Burl. "About this time yesterday I ate a can of cold beans. I didn't eat since."

The man turned, leaned on the piano. "Then I take it your mother isn't going to be phoning, complaining that I've ruined your appetite."

Burl averted his eyes, hurriedly ate another mouthful. "We don't have a phone," he said.

"That's just as well," said the man. "Because neither do *we*."

He turned his back again. He held his right wrist in his left hand, and Burl could see that he was counting. He seemed to be taking his pulse.

Burl concentrated on his eggs. The man had said "we," but it did not seem possible that another person shared this cabin with him.

Alone now at the table, his attention freed from his host's penetrating gaze, Burl noticed a letter lying open. "Dear Nog," it began. Under the letter lay an envelope addressed to Nathaniel Gow. But the letter had not been sent here. It was addressed to the Plaza Hotel in New York City. Then Burl noticed a brown cardigan hanging over the back of the chair at the desk. The initials N.O.G. were embroidered in gold on the pocket.

Burl laid down his fork. Nog still had his back to him. He dared to look at the letter again. The return address was from Toronto, from "R. Corngold." Burl flipped to the end of the letter. "Take care, Reggie."

"I propose a test," said Nog suddenly. "I suppose it would be more appropriate to propose a toast, since it's suppertime, but I don't drink, so it will have to be a test, instead."

"Pardon?"

"If you were a body of water, what would you be?" he asked. "It's another game. Would you be a lake? The Indian Ocean? A nice hot soapy bath? What?"

< 4 1 >

Burl was at sea. Games were something you did at recess when the weather was bad. Mrs. Agnew liked word games, but Burl had never encountered a game outside of school. What were the rules here? What happened if you guessed wrong?

"Well?" said Nog. "No, wait a minute—'well' doesn't count, even though it is a body of water. We've had quite enough 'wells' in this conversation. 'Well' this and 'well' that. I'll make a note to myself to eradicate from my vocabulary the use of the word 'well' as an interjection from this moment on." He paused. "What, then?"

Burl was as ready as he'd ever be. "A stream?"

Nog walked toward his guest, his fingers pressed together, looking pleased. "What kind of a stream?"

"A trout stream, fast moving but with deep pools."

"Bravo," said Nog.

"What would you be?"

Nog wagged his finger. "I'm the master of ceremonies. I do the asking." He took the chair from the worktable and dragged it over to the eating table. He sat down, crossed his legs. He looked hard at Burl, until Burl turned away. When he spoke again, his voice had lost its singsong, excited quality.

"If your father were a wild animal, what would he be?"

Burl wrapped his arms more tightly around himself. He was still shirtless, and the room was cooling down as evening advanced.

Nog's eyes narrowed. "That scar on your shoulder, the bruise on your lower rib cage, the burn marks—cigarette?— on your arm ... I think some kind of ferocious animal did this."

Burl stared at his empty plate. With his finger he wiped up a smear of grease, tasted it.

"Is there room here, just for tonight?" he asked.

< 4 2 >

Nog dragged his hand down the length of his face, distorting his features. The whites of his eyes were veined in red.

Burl could see No written all over his face. He had heard the word enough times to recognize the signs, the shape the face takes on just before saying No.

"I don't think that would be a practical idea," said Nog. He got up a little unsteadily from his chair and padded in his stocking feet over to the piano stool, on which he perched, his legs folded, looking out at the lake.

Burl slumped in his chair. He had allowed himself to relax, allowed the tiredness to climb up his limbs from his aching feet. Somehow he would have to push that aching weariness back down now, regain what strength he could muster. But where would he go?

"I just hoped—"

"What did you hope?"

"Just for tonight. I'll go first thing in the morning."

"Where?"

"It doesn't matter."

Nog didn't speak for a moment. "Who are you?" he said at last.

"Burl."

"Burl who?"

"Burl ... Burl Crow." There, he had told him.

"Look at me, Burl Crow."

Burl looked up.

"You don't know who I am?"

Burl's eyes wandered to the envelope that lay between them on the table.

"I guess you're him," he said, pointing at the name on the address.

"But you've never heard of Nathaniel Orlando Gow?"

Burl shook his head.

< 4 3 >

"Did you or did you not follow me here to pry into my private life?" His voice was raised, like a prosecutor in some movie bearing down on an evasive witness.

"No! I don't even know where *here* is."

There was a long pause. Burl didn't dare look up. He got up from his chair. His shirt hung on a hook by the door. He took it down and began to put it on.

Nog turned on the table lamp at his desk. He took a pencil from the cup and held it poised above a blank page. Then he put it down and started patting his chest pockets, inside and out, looking for his glasses. They were on the kitchen counter. Burl picked them up and took them to him. The lenses were greasy. He cleaned them off on his shirt.

"Thank you," said Nog.

"Thanks for supper," said Burl.

Nog was bent over his work. "It was nothing."

At the door Burl stopped. "Say good-bye to the baron and Sir Chauncey for me," he said.

Nog smiled, even though he didn't look up. Then he put down his pencil firmly on the table and leaned back in his chair, sticking out his long legs in front of him.

"In my business," he said, "we have a little something called 'take two.' Do you know what that is?"

Burl found himself thinking of supper at home, where he was usually told to take just one. "No."

"When you are onstage playing the piano, if you make a mistake—then you make a mistake and nothing can be done about it. Perfection is not possible on the concert stage. I'm rather keen on perfection myself. And that's why I don't play live anymore. Are you following me so far?"

Burl nodded. He even dared to inch back into the room away from the door. Nog's voice was all singsong again and sociable.

< 4 4 >

"In the recording studio, however, if you're playing a sonata, let's say, and you get to a sticky part and play a bad note or a note that's too loud or just plain wonky, you can simply stop. And then do you know what you do?"

"You take two?"

"Absolutely. You take two. You play the difficult passage over again and plunk it in the sonata and there it is. Perfection—thanks to the miracle of the recording studio."

Burl thought about this a moment. "Isn't that kind of cheating?" he asked.

"Argh!" said Nog, throwing his hands up in torment. "Even the woods are filled with critics! Do you really think, Master Burl, that art is like a game of football? That the dropped pass must forever remain dropped? The fumble cannot be scooped up and placed back in the hands of the otherwise competent fullback? Nonsense. And that, you see, is the problem with live concerts. They are like some dreadful sports event: the noisy crowd, the fumbles, having to play when you're sick as a dog. That's not art."

He grabbed a piece of music from the stack piled neatly on the table and pointed to it. "This," he said, "is art. All the notes and the arrangement in which they are to be played. A performance that is less than what the composer wrote is not art. Do you see my point, Burl?"

Burl nodded carefully. "I get it," he said.

"Good," said Nog. He took a deep breath. "Then let's try it out, shall we?"

"Pardon?"

"Take two." Nog jumped to his feet, rubbing his hands together. "Sit down at the table," he said. "Go on. That's right. Exactly where you were before. Good. Now—how did you put it?"

"Put what?"

< 4 5 >

" 'Is there room here for me?' Is that what you said?"

Burl began to feel slightly more optimistic. "Yes," he said. "Just for tonight."

"Uh-uh-uh," said Nog, shaking his finger. "Not so fast. You must knock first."

"I have to knock?"

"Yes," said Nog. "Kind of like in a story where the hero stands before a magic door, and he must rap on it three times if he expects it to open. That kind of thing." He rapped on the table top. *Knock, knock, knock.*

Burl looked at him. The man looked serious, and there was an eagerness in his eyes that shone through the strain and tiredness. Burl squeezed his eyes shut and rapped three times. *Knock, knock, knock.*

He opened his eyes hopefully. Nog was staring at him sternly.

"You knocked?"

Burl cleared his throat. "Is there room for me here?" he said. "Just for tonight."

Nog stepped back as if in astonishment. Now his face was half in shadows. "Haven't we been through this?"

Burl felt light-headed. "Yeah. But I'm supposed to pretend that it turns out different."

Nog scratched his chin. He frowned. "What a remarkable idea."

"It's already working, sort of. You said something different."

Nog stepped forward and leaned on the table. "But I didn't say you could stay, did I? So it isn't all that different."

Burl's bright prospect expired. Just like that. This man was nuts. He was amusing himself, like a cat with a chipmunk.

"All right!" said Burl, shoving himself away from the table. He glared at Nog. "Thanks for the meal. I'm sorry for coming here."

< 4 6 >

He opened the door.

"Burl," said Nog, raising his voice.

Burl stopped in the open doorway. It was cold outside. Night. "I didn't mean to disturb you."

"Perhaps not, but I am disturbed nonetheless. I disturb easily. I have spent a lot of time escaping from people who wish to disturb me. But what really disturbs me is how quickly you have given up."

"Given up?" Burl felt a new wave of exhaustion overtake him. "I *tried* take two," he said.

"Ah," said Nog. "The name of the game is misleading. Sometimes, in my business, take two becomes take six or take six hundred. Sometimes the door opens to a wizard, sometimes to an ogre. Perfection is really nothing more nor less than getting the results you desire. That is never a simple business."

Burl leaned against the doorway. "Yeah. I guess." And with that he closed the door.

He stood for a moment on the deck, invigorated by the cool, clean night air, the simple song of the crickets and frogs. The certainty of moonlight. He breathed in deeply—once, twice, three times. He thought of the cave by the cliff, of gathering pine needles to sleep on, leaves and grass and moss to cover himself.

Then he turned around and rapped firmly on the cabin door. *Knock, knock, knock.*

It opened immediately.

< 4 7 >

The Maestro

THE ELECTRICAL POWER for the cabin came from a diesel generator housed in a shed set a good distance back from the lakefront, out of earshot.

Even though there was a good long stone's throw of bush between the two buildings, the shed was well insulated for sound. Burl didn't hear the engine until he was at the door fumbling with the handle, with a bag of garbage in each hand and a pocket flashlight clenched between his teeth. He had offered to clean up, and there was a garbage can in the shed. The single can had been full for some time, and the shed was crowded with bulging garbage bags, some of which had spilled their contents onto the concrete floor, where bits and pieces were left over from the construction of the camp. Odd-shaped scraps of lumber, cans of paint,

< 4 8 >

roofing tiles, and boxes of nails were piled all higgledy-piggledy.

By flashlight Burl read the letter he had slipped into his pocket when he was cleaning up the cabin.

Dear Nog:

So you have wormed your way into the Big Apple again! How goes the battle? Are they treating you right at the studio? Is Mr. Gibbons easy to get along with this time around? I can't wait to hear.

Toronto is breathing a sigh of relief since you left. For one thing, it's truly quiet at night now without you driving around, the Top 40 blasting from your car radio. Such bad taste! Really, you ought to be ashamed.

For another thing, it's infinitely easier to get work done here at the old Canadian Broadcorping Castration. You're far too interesting—that's your problem. Here I am, a senior producer trying to work, and there you are being interesting well into the night. Think, Nog—this is the CBC: nobody is paid around here to be interesting!

All kidding aside, I love your idea for a new show, and you can bet I'll put in a good word for it at the Big Annual Meeting. (Frankly, it's a shoo-in; Bernie loves it already. And anyway, despite what I said above, we all miss our favorite ghost slip-sliding around the halls at night. Miss him a lot.)

Anyhow—my work waits. Please give me a call when you're back. What am I saying—you call way too much. You support the phone company all by yourself! I mean a proper visit—in person—and not at three in the morning, either. Be a reasonable chap and come around for a meal. In case you didn't know, that's what reasonable chaps do.

Take care,
Reggie

The letter was six months old. Burl wondered what it had been doing out on the table. He slipped it back into his pocket. He closed the shed.

< 4 9 >

Burl stopped as soon as he had made his way out into the clearing where the cabin stood. He clicked off the flashlight. How different the night looked to him, knowing that he had somewhere to stay. Nog had given him a clean shirt and a pair of pants. The pants were baggy, but they were dry and clean. And the shirt was the color of putty but finer and softer than any material Burl had ever felt against his skin. Viyella, it said on the tag. There was a tiny gold N.O.G. embroidered on the pocket.

The moon was high now. He heard Nog playing the piano, something very slow, serene. Burl wondered if this was the effect of the drugs. He had watched Nog take some pills out of a flight bag he kept by his mattress. Burl knew about pills.

A splash caught his attention. A dark shape swam across the head of the bay, leaving a silver wake. A beaver. There was a big lodge to the west. Walking down to the water's edge, Burl could see the outline of the cliff that marked the eastern head of the bay. He thought of himself curling up in the cave there on a mattress of pine needles with no more blankets than he could manufacture from grass and moss. How far the day had brought him.

Back in the cabin, Nog had turned off the lights and lit candles on the tables and on the piano. The one nearest the door almost guttered when Burl entered. A chilly wind snuck past him into the room.

Nog shivered and stopped playing. He looked up with some surprise, as if he had forgotten all about his houseguest.

"Can you play the piano?" he asked, his voice sedated.

"No, sir."

"Please, don't call me sir. Call me Baron, if you like. No, I don't feel like a baron anymore. Nathaniel. Better still, call me Maestro. Yes, I like that. What do you think?"

"Maestro," said Burl. "That's like a conductor?"

< 5 0 >

"Oh, more than just a conductor. Master. Teacher. Here, I'll teach you something. Then you'll *have* to call me Maestro."

"I can't."

"Nonsense. Come."

Burl washed his hands in the soapy water where he'd left the dirty dishes to soak. There were quite a few. They'd need a lot of soaking.

"I'll teach you one tiny bit of my new piece," said the Maestro.

Obediently, Burl presented his freshly cleaned hands. The teacher seemed amused. He pressed each finger, as if they were made of putty, into the proper location on the keyboard. "Quietly," he said. Burl pressed down. The sound leaped into the darkened room. He pulled his fingers back in alarm.

"That's the first chord of the 'Silence in Heaven,'" the Maestro whispered. He took Burl's hands again and moved his fingers until he had played four such chords. "Now again," he said. Burl watched the keyboard steadily while the man moved his hands as if he, Burl, were a puppet and the Maestro were his puppeteer. Finally, after several rehearsals, Burl tried the four chords by himself.

"Ever so quiet," said the Maestro. "The passage is called 'Silence in Heaven,' not 'Bowling Tournament in Heaven.'"

Burl wanted to stop playing. His fingers ached, but mostly he was afraid of doing it wrong. No—it wasn't that. It was the pressure of wanting so much to get it right.

"Hold each chord for a count of four." The Maestro pointed to the whole notes on the sheet of music, but Burl only glanced up for a second, for as soon as his eyes left the keys, his fingers lost their places. Besides, the pencil marks scribbled on the paper meant nothing to him.

"There's been a lot of crashing around in the piece up to here," said the Maestro. "The choir has been booming. So this

< 5 1 >

is a kind of breather for the audience. The strings will play it alone."

Burl played the progression of four chords as quietly as he could, but this time the music seemed to resonate all around them. The Maestro smiled mischievously. He had his foot on the loud pedal.

"It's an oratorio," he said. "Do you know what that is?"

Burl shook his head. He played his little piece again and again, his tongue firmly fixed between his teeth. Then, as quickly as it had begun, the lesson was over. Though the Maestro did not say anything, Burl felt his impatience to get back to work, and he reluctantly pulled his fingers away from the silky smoothness of the keyboard. But he did not stop looking at the keys. And with his eyes he memorized the paths his fingers had taken to make the sounds.

"What's an oratorio?" he asked.

"It's an excuse to make a lot of noise," said the Maestro, his voice sluggish now. "No, I'm kidding. It's a dramatic work, usually on a religious theme, with an orchestra and choir and soloists—the whole shooting match—but, unlike an opera, the singers don't have to act. Which is just as well, really, because most singers *can't* act."

Burl was still sitting at the piano, admiring it in the yellow puddles of light the candles spilled over the keys.

"It's a great toy," said the Maestro. Standing, he played a rapid arpeggio at the high end. Burl immediately gave up his seat. His teacher slid behind the piano without lifting his fingers from the keyboard. He seemed oblivious to Burl. Then he said, "Can you imagine what you could do with this thing with the right-sized outboard motor?" Burl laughed and returned to his dishwashing.

"I'll drive," said the Maestro. He played what might have

< 5 2 >

been a motor revving up. A very elegant motor. "You can water-ski behind."

It was almost dark in the kitchen corner. Burl didn't mind. The dishwater was hot and soothing. He felt filled with calmness.

He heard the Maestro shiver.

"I could plug in the heater," said Burl. The Maestro said nothing, but nodded. Burl had noticed the electric heater earlier when he was looking the place over. From a corner he dragged it out, then plugged it in and placed it under the piano. He had already noticed there was no woodstove.

"It must get pretty wicked in here in the winter," he said.

"I can assure you, Master Crow, I *never* intend to find out."

Burl stopped washing for a minute and let his hands just sit in the dishwater. It penetrated him and dug out the bone-chilling memory of the night before, the rain-filled shack. He allowed his thoughts to drift into a dream. This place, empty all winter.

"I like the *idea* of winter," said the Maestro as he played. "I like the purity of it. I'm sure winter is the perfect cure."

"For what?" asked Burl. The Maestro didn't answer right away. He was caught up in a passage of music. Then he stopped.

"For everything," he said at last.

< 5 3 >

The Intruder

BURL LAY IN THE SHADOWS that gathered at the end of the piano. The Maestro had given him a pillow and a couple of blankets. The corner behind the piano and beside the door seemed the most out-of-the-way place for him to stay. It was plain that Nathaniel Orlando Gow composed by night.

"I don't like to see the sun rise," he said.

Burl, tired as he was, couldn't quite fall asleep.

"Are you famous?" he asked.

The man looked up from his desk. "Tremendously famous," he said. "All over the world. *Horribly* famous."

He got up and rooted around in the cupboard under the sink for another box of Arrowroots. It was the only thing Burl had seen him eat.

"Is it horrible, being famous?"

The Maestro chewed thoughtfully. "There's only one thing

< 5 4 >

harder than being famous," he said. "And that is being Nathaniel Orlando Gow."

He carried his box of cookies to the piano, where he picked up one of the candles and blew the other one out. He resettled himself at his writing desk.

"You don't have to stop playing for me," said Burl.

"No," said the Maestro. "But I do have to stop playing if I'm to begin working." He yawned, but his movements, fast and jerky, showed no signs of drowsiness. He had taken more pills. He put on his glasses and started writing by candlelight. He leaned down close to the surface of the table.

"This bit at the beginning is all flies and heat," he said. He was talking to the music. "Flies and heat and visions. Here I am in the freezing northern woods writing about visions in the Greek islands."

He mumbled on like this in sporadic bursts. His voice was slurred. This was the drugs, Burl was sure. He had heard his mother's voice grow lazy like this.

Burl began to drift off, then awoke again, for the Maestro's voice had risen.

"I've been farther north than this, you know. Right up to James Bay. It's impossibly beautiful. No trees to get in the way. Vast. Scary as sin. And that was only in summer. I still have not experienced the *dark* of a winter in the north. I don't think I'm ready for it. This lake is my compromise. A glimpse of the Big Dark, as it were, if not the whole thing." He picked up his pen again.

Burl remembered catching the morning school bus in Pharaoh in the pitch-black dead of winter. He left school in the same darkness.

"It gets very dark here," he said.

The Maestro bent to his writing with renewed attention, his hand curling awkwardly.

< 5 5 >

We're both left-handed, thought Burl. He turned on his side so that he could see out the huge sail of a window. It was alive with stars.

Burl dreamed of the rainbow trout he had caught at his father's secret place. It would have been nice to mount that trout on some lacquered plank of wood, arching with the lure still in its mouth, still fighting.

"This was the fish I was catching," he imagined saying to someone. The phrase hung in the dream air, the middle of a conversation. What was he talking about? To whom?

Suddenly it was his father looking up at the mounted fish above the mantel. "I seen that fish before. That fish is mine!" he said, grabbing Burl by the collar. "You stole that from me." He shook his son, and though it was only a dream, Burl felt the room shake around him.

Thwack!

The old man was hitting him.

Thwack!

And a third time. Burl twisted and turned. He had to wake up, get away. He bumped into something hard and woke up wrapped around the leg of the piano. Then he heard a whimpering sound that wasn't him or his dream father. It came from the other side of sleep. He sat up.

The Maestro was standing behind his writing desk, his face underlit by the low candles. Horror-struck. From behind Burl there was a creaking sound, followed by a blast against the cabin wall. Something at the door.

Burl was on his knees in a flash. It was his father—that was his first thought—breaking down the door with an ax. Then there was another blast, and though the Maestro whimpered again, this time Burl was awake enough to recognize the sound for what it was. He scrambled out from under the

< 5 6 >

piano. He approached the door. There it was again. A thump that rattled the doorknob, followed by a scratching sound. A grunt. With the heels of both hands, Burl pounded on the door, shouting a loud curse.

The creature on the other side backed away, moved across the deck. Burl rushed to the lakeside window, and there it was, a deeper blackness than the night, a bear. The Maestro saw it, too. It was sniffing at the glass, rising on its hind legs, poking at the glass with its long claws.

"Oh, Christ!" The Maestro sat down with a thud, his arms wrapped around his chest as if to hold himself together.

Turning toward him, Burl saw the paperweight rocks on the desk. He raced across the room, grabbing the two largest. He headed toward the door.

"No!" he heard the Maestro say, but by then he had flung open the door and stepped outside.

"Shoo!" he cried. "Shoo!"

The bear turned, stepped toward the noise, squinting near-sightedly, sniffing the air. Burl hurled one of the rocks. It missed the bear and clattered across the deck. The bear ran off a couple of paces and warily circled the lone deck chair.

"Get out of here!" Burl yelled. He moved toward it, stamping his foot. He heard a voice behind him, pleading with him to close the door.

The deck was cold on Burl's bare feet. The bear stepped out from behind the chair. Burl heaved the second rock. It hit the bear on the side.

In two strides the animal reached the railing, and with a speed that seemed improbable for such a lumbering huge creature, it tore off, only stopping when it was on the beach.

Burl clapped his hands loudly, but the bear stood its ground.

The Maestro was at the door. He handed Burl a third stone as big as an orange. Burl stealthily made his way down the

< 5 7 >

steps to the shore, his eyes never leaving his adversary, ready to run back at any moment. His toes gripped the wet earth. He felt every root and pebble.

The bear lifted its nose in the air. It made as if to return, took a step up the shore. A second step. Reconsidered, turned away. It was then, with the bear's flank as a target, that Burl summoned all his strength and launched the third stone. It hit the animal in the head.

With a dreadful grunt the bear turned on its heels toward the water. In great loping strides it plunged into the lake until it was swimming across the bay. Burl watched it regain the land at the beaver lodge and tear off into the bush. He waited a full minute until the crashing progress through the underbrush had faded to nothing, and the only sound left was the song of a wood thrush. Morning was coming.

He marched back to the cabin, shaking. Out of the corner of his eye he saw a trail of empty cans and crusts, a jam jar, a chocolate-bar wrapper. The trail stretched back into the woods in the direction of the shed.

He would have to deal with that soon, he thought, but not now. Not yet.

< 5 8 >

The Book of Revelation

"WHAT AM I DOING HERE?" The maestro had collapsed on his mattress. Burl, wearing one of his host's heavy overcoats, was busy making coffee. "This is utterly ridiculous, insane. Do you think I'm insane, Master Burl?"

Burl brought him a cup of coffee. The man sat up, looked at him through eyes that brimmed more with outrage than with fear.

"I don't know how you take it," said Burl.

"I don't know, either."

"I mean the coffee," said Burl.

The Maestro took the coffee black. He wrapped his fingers tightly around it as if to squeeze the warmth right out of it.

Already the sun was poking its own long translucent fingers through the trees on the eastern rim of the lake.

"Do you need one of your pills?" Burl asked.

< 5 9 >

The Maestro stared at him. "*One* of them?" He laughed a little hysterically, coughed, and nodded.

Burl crawled across the unslept-in bed to the shoulder bag. The inside was like a medicine cabinet. He had never seen so many drugs. He read the labels by the gray light seeping in the window.

"The Fiorinal," said the Maestro. Burl took out the Fiorinal. "And the Valium." Burl found the Valium.

The Maestro took a couple of each, swallowed some of his coffee, stood up, and made his way to the worktable. The candles had guttered while the door was open. He switched on the table lamp and sat at the mess on his desk.

"I'm a lunatic, Burl."

"Maybe." Burl sat at the piano. "My mother eats those Valium ones like candy."

The Maestro scowled. "I gather by that, that your mother is trying to escape this weary world."

"I guess so," said Burl.

"Then we do not share much in common, your mother and I. For I am merely trying, against all the odds, to *stay* in this weary world."

Burl looked down. He hadn't meant to be rude.

"Bears are more afraid of us than we are of them," he said.

"Don't be so sure," said the Maestro. He had been looking through a fat briefcase on the floor, and now he drew from it a weird piece of rubbery equipment that Burl at first thought might be an instrument but then realized was the little sleeve and pump that a doctor used to check blood pressure.

The Maestro strapped the sleeve to his arm and pumped it up. With a watch he recorded the change in his heart rate as he let out the air.

"I'm a very sick man," he said.

"Mostly," said Burl, "my mother's just sick and tired."

< 6 0 >

"Well, yes ... there is that."

Burl tried to imagine his mother. Asleep? Alone? He didn't want to think about it.

A moment passed. Burl drank some coffee. A white-throated sparrow sang. Somewhere across the lake a loon called.

"It was my fault," said Burl. "I should have been more careful with the garbage."

"No," said the Maestro. "You are not to blame. In truth, I'm out of my element here. A boy-of-the-woods like you must think me a complete nincompoop living here like this. And you'd be right. I am a shrewd businessman, Burl. A canny Scot by birth and inclination. I do not throw money away, though I have a great deal of it. This cabin—this rustic temple—is my folly. Do you know what a folly is? It's a building meant to satisfy an elaborate fantasy. It is, in short, the work of a fool. I am no more equipped to live here than that beast out there would be equipped to live in Toronto. He, at least, would be able to find himself some dinner. I would starve in a minute if it weren't for my monthly airlift. And I have a man come up by train every other week to hook up the next drum of diesel fuel and generally do for me whatever needs to be done."

Burl shifted uneasily in his seat. "Why don't you go back to Toronto? Are you in trouble there?"

The Maestro smiled at him, and it was perhaps the sweetest smile Burl had seen yet. There hadn't been all that many.

"I am only in whatever trouble I cook up for myself," he said. "And, as you have experienced, I am not much of a cook."

"Supper was great," said Burl.

"Nonsense. Let's call a scrambled egg a scrambled egg. Besides, I wasn't really talking about that kind of cooking."

The Maestro picked up the sheet of music he had been working on. "This is my crack at immortality," he said.

< 6 1 >

Burl crossed the room to look at the music. "Song of Victory" was scrawled in capitals across the top. "Is this the oratorio?"

"Part of it."

It looked to Burl like a bunch of dots and lines flying all over the page. "Couldn't you do this in Toronto?"

The Maestro took the sheet of music from him. "I left Toronto to escape the Shadow. The Shadow is phone calls and luncheon meetings and people still wanting me to come out of retirement and perform in Santiago or teach in New York or lecture in Moscow or just show up at a party and look like a composer. The Shadow is *disturbance*. It is the beast that keeps me away from writing this. And it's far more persistent than our visitor tonight."

He replaced the sheets of music on one of the piles on his desk. He neatened the sides.

"You'll need some new rocks," said Burl.

The Maestro chuckled. "I've got enough up here," he said, tapping himself on the skull. He looked past Burl out at the gathering dawn. His eyes squinted.

"A man on a train told me about this lake," he said, leaning forward in his chair now, the fires in his eyes relit. "He heard about it from an archaeologist. This spot was on a native portage route. This very beach was a campsite ten thousand years ago. Think of it. They have found arrowheads and flint tools right here.

"The man on the train was a prospector. He had staked a mining claim here, but he didn't really expect to find anything. Not gold or silver or anything more precious than he could see with his naked eye. He just fell in love with the natural beauty of the place. When he told me it was on the CPR train route, just a good healthy half-hour walk in—Mile 29, he called it—well, I knew I had to see it. But when I actually

<6 2 >

came here, I knew that what I needed more than health, more even than the quiet, was the solitude. I was sure that only in utter isolation would I be able to see what Saint John saw, though I daresay this is a far cry from his hot little Greek island."

The Maestro dug out a book from the litter before him. It was the Bible.

"Do you know your Bible?"

Burl shook his head.

"The Book of Revelation. Wild stuff," said the Maestro enthusiastically. "Last book in the New Testament. As if anything could follow it. It's written by someone named John, who may or may not be John the Apostle—there are far too many Johns in the Bible. He was exiled for being a Christian to a small island called Patmos. I love that name. I'm thinking of calling the opening movement 'Patmospheres.' Do you get it?"

Burl wasn't sure. The Maestro frowned.

"Anyway, back to the exiled John. Are you a Christian, Burl?"

"My grandmother is."

"How clever of her. It's quite a juggling act. All those truths you have to hold on to at once. I'm not sure I'm up to it, but it makes for a fabulous story."

"A revelation," said Burl. "Is that like when you see into the future?"

"Yes, prophecy. The Greek word is 'apocalypse.' John's apocalypse is a fabulous dream about the end of the world. Armageddon, the battlefield where the kings of the lower world are gathered together by the beast and the dragon and the Antichrist—I use a lot of trombones for them—to do battle with Christ. So there's this war in heaven, and a lament after the fall of Babylon and then a 'Song of Victory' as all the

< 6 3 >

good guys get to go to the New Jerusalem in heaven. It's got everything."

Burl went to the piano and played the progression of chords he had learned. "And this is in it?"

The Maestro looked over the top of his glasses, which had slipped down his nose.

"Amazing," he said. "What a marvelous teacher you must have. That's the quiet in heaven just after the lamb breaks the seventh seal. In the Bible the silence lasts half an hour. I'm tempted to make the audience sit through a half hour of silence, but I'll allow myself to be talked out of that." He started to hum. Stopped, his lips pursed.

"This is to be my Handel's *Messiah*. There will be massed choirs, an orchestra so large there won't be a single good fiddle player out of work in all of Canada, and me at the organ pulling out all the stops. What do you think?"

"It sounds awesome."

"Yes, precisely. Awesome. Except for one thing, Burl. I've got to finish writing it first."

An involuntary muscle spasm made its way down the Maestro's right cheek. His eyes filled with a kind of sorrow that seemed to leap across the space between the man and the boy.

"I didn't know," said Burl.

"Know what?"

"How important it was. Being alone here. I've wrecked it."

"Wrecked it? I'll say you wrecked it. You saved my useless life."

"But you're not useless! You're going to write this acopolit, acropol—this oratorio. And then you'll be even more famous."

The Maestro leaned so far forward that his chin rested on the table. "Yes, " he said. "And then the next child who stumbles out of the woods into my life will be sure to know of the immortal Nathaniel Orlando Gow."

< 6 4 >

Burl felt foolish. "I don't know hardly anything."

The Maestro straightened up in his chair. "You scared off that hairy thing, and for that I owe you a debt of gratitude."

"Any fool can scare off a bear," said Burl. "You just make a lot of noise. But you make music. That's a lot harder."

The Maestro was not listening. "Tonight's episode convinces me I must get back to civilization."

"What about the oratorio?"

"Hmm? Oh, that. I have almost a full first sketch. The only thing that needs a lot of work is the 'Seven Trumpets' bit, which is when all the pestilence and plagues and fires happen. You've heard of the Four Horsemen of the Apocalypse? No, of course you haven't. You are a wild child raised in the woods by wolves. What do you know of anything."

He sounded vexed, disappointed. As if he thought he had been talking to someone who understood what he was saying.

Burl finished off the dregs of his coffee. He swiveled in his chair to look out the window. A light mist rose like cold fire from the folds and creases of the forest. In the bay, a merganser paddled by with a brood of ducklings. Twelve, thirteen—too many to be all her own. Sometimes a pike or a snapping turtle got a mother.

The Maestro sighed deeply, closed his eyes. "I'm so very tired." He got up from his desk, crawled across his mattress, and searched through the medicine bag. "Tired of the whole thing." He popped something into his mouth.

He heaved himself to his feet, yawned, and stretched. He stood at the window next to where Burl sat stoop-shouldered, looking out at the mists burning off the water. As he watched, the sun appeared above the eastern rim of the trees, a white ghost of a thing.

"I don't know how you found me," said the Maestro, "but I think I'm almost glad you did."

< 6 5 >

Burl swallowed hard. "I'll clean up that mess outside," he said.

"Good for you."

The Maestro's voice was already distant, pulling away. He pulled a string and released an opaque black curtain that covered half the window. From the other side he released a second curtain that blocked out the lake from view. Then he proceeded to the other two windows, until the room was reduced to the mean little glow of the electric light he had turned on at his desk when his candles had burned out.

"I hate to see the sun rise," he said.

< 6 6 >

The Ogre

IT WAS GOOD TO get outside. The air was cool, and a wind from the east was already picking up, making the aspens tremble, ruffling the mirror surface of the bay, and blowing the mist away.

Burl quickly went about cleaning up after the bear. The path to the shed was littered with garbage. The shed door had been clawed open; the inside was a mess. He emptied it completely and discovered a hammerhead with a broken section of handle still in it. He could use it to make a plate to strengthen the door. Then, when there was time, he could carve a new handle.

If he were to stay, there were many chores that needed attention. Something would have to be done about the garbage. Burnable things would have to be burned; cans would have to be washed clean of scent and squashed flat. Leftovers would

< 6 7 >

have to be taken to some distant spot, preferably an island—
he had seen islands from the cliff top—but, in any case, a
long way from the cabin.

Burl stopped working long enough to imagine hauling his
old canoe up here somehow. It was under wrap and in need
of repair in the shed out back of his father's house. It seemed
impossible he could ever get back there. And yet this beautiful
lake was at Mile 29—that's what the Maestro had said. Pharaoh was at Mile 10. The CPR track went pretty well due
north out of Pharaoh and then curved west. North by northwest
had led him across the base of a triangle joining these two
places. Not such a distance and yet so far away, it seemed.

The chill air made him shiver, and he got back to work.
He was pleased that there would be something for him to do
for as long as he was here.

When the shed was shipshape, Burl searched through the
used paint cans until he found one with some creosote in it.
He had noticed that the posts under the deck were coated in
the thick black coal tar. With a crusty old paintbrush he
smeared the largest piece of plywood he could find. Then he
placed it just inside the door with the garbage bags behind it.
When the bear came sniffing for treats, he would get a nose
full of creosote instead. It might keep him from exploring any
farther.

Satisfied with the job he had done, Burl locked the shed.
There had been a padlock all along. It was sitting on a shelf,
the key still in it. Burl pocketed the key. The shed would be
his responsibility.

The door seemed quite sturdy. Maybe later with his refur-
bished hammer he would fix the bear's damage to the cabin
door with some scrap wood and nails. He found himself
thinking of the natives who had made tools on this beach ten
thousand years earlier.

< 6 8 >

He combed the beach. The sun had burned a hole in the mist. It would be a good clear day. Out on the bay he saw something swimming toward the shore. A mink, with a fish in its mouth. The mink saw Burl, too, and, dropping its breakfast in the shallows, it snaked over the rocky shore and slipped quietly into the bush. Burl splashed through the water to the dead fish. It was a sucker, a chunky one with its head already gone.

Burl suddenly remembered his twice-stolen lure. It was back in the cabin. And there was bailing wire in the shed. He could catch a fish. Make the Maestro a real meal and make himself indispensable while he was at it. He raced back to the cabin, entering it very quietly.

The genius twitched but did not awaken. When Burl had his Brazen Wiggler, he grabbed himself some cheese and a heel of bread. He took a pocketful of plums as well, and a can of soda. The Maestro's borrowed pants had deep pockets.

He got the bailing wire from the shed and then followed the beach out toward the beaver lodge. The lodge would be near deep water. Maybe there would be a perch hole there, maybe some bass.

But before he reached the dam, he came to a spot where a creek emptied into the bay. There was a tumble of rocks, boulders the size of small cars, standing sentry at the creek head. A big fish would like the water there, deep and clear. The rocks made a cool hiding spot for a fish to wait for what shuffled down the creek. A juicy crayfish, maybe; an even juicier bullfrog.

Burl found his way to the top of a boulder and sat cross-legged, preparing his gear. The sun on his back filled him with warmth. He had found a hand-sized piece of wood into which he cut notches at either end with his pocketknife. He tied the bailing wire onto the wood and wound it on the way you

<69>

wind a kite string onto its spool. Then he tied on the Brazen Wiggler.

There were blueberry bushes growing up behind him. He snacked on the few berries he could find so late in the season. Then, looking up for another mouthful, he saw a fat black caterpillar with a red stripe down its back. Carefully he pulled it away from the bush. He looked at it in his hand. It was a lot prettier than a worm. He hooked it onto his lure. What fish could resist such a meal?

Burl lowered his line into the water and settled down to wait. His father had said that the time you spent fishing was free, didn't count in the reckoning of your life span. If you totaled up the hours you spent with a baited line in the water, you could just add those hours on to the end of your life and spin it out a bit longer. At first Burl thought his father had made this up. Then he saw the same idea woodburned on a sign in the Woolworth. Still, the waiting was good with a cheese sandwich filling up your belly and the sun beginning to cook the shivers out of you. Burl got a little sleepy. The morning wore on.

The fish hammered the bait like thunder. Pow! The hand line almost jumped from his grasp. He grabbed on to it hard and with both hands began to spool in his line.

The fish leaped from the water. A big bass, blond-skinned from swimming in such a sandy reach. It jumped again. Burl was sure he would lose it, but the lure was in deep. If he could just hold on. If he'd had his rod he would have given the fish some slack, let it run, wear itself out, but he couldn't do that. It jumped a third time, vomiting up a frog.

Burl scrambled down the rock to a ledge nearer the water. While he was making his way down, the bass swam deep and under a submerged log. At the last second, Burl saw the ploy and pulled the fish away from the log. Then he tugged and

< 7 0 >

tugged and muscled it in. Reaching down, he grabbed the fish by its lower jaw, his thumb in its mouth.

It was big and strong, wet dynamite. He wasted no time getting it to the safety of the shore, up in the rough grass, fearing that with one powerful leap such a creature might make good its escape even now.

He tied three strands of bailing wire through its mouth until he was sure it was secure. Then he waded out into the bay and let the fish back down into its watery home. He must keep it alive, fresh until he filleted it. It swam beside him like an angry dog on a leash. He didn't walk fast, didn't want to drown his catch.

As he approached the cabin, the Maestro stepped out onto the deck in his coats, though by now the sun was high. He watched Burl approach, but the boy held in his excitement and waited until he was at the deck before he spoke.

"Got something for your breakfast," he said. He hauled his trophy out of the drink. It flapped in his grasp, gasping for breath. He stared at it himself, admiring the muscled beauty of the creature glinting in the sun.

The Maestro looked away. He was looking out over the water, his hair—what there was of it—riffled by the breeze off the lake. Burl glanced quickly to see what in the world could possibly be more appealing than this miracle of flesh.

There was nothing. Only the lake, mistless now, clear.

"Yes, well," said the Maestro without looking at him. "I guess that's about the last straw."

Burl waded ashore. He stood at the bottom of the steps, breathing hard.

"This setting is far too distracting to work in," said the Maestro. No good-morning. No congratulatory smile. He seemed to be having trouble getting his breath. "What was I

< 7 1 >

thinking," he mumbled. "What on *earth* was I thinking." He leaned against the railing.

"Are you okay?"

"I was."

"It's a smallmouth bass," said Burl. "I caught it with some bailing wire I found in the shed." He thought maybe an explanation might help the Maestro to see the wonder of it. But he only stared at the fish, and then, with eyes that frosted over, he scrutinized Burl.

"I'm almost entirely a vegetarian," he said. "A fact you obviously had not noticed. I have a great affinity for animals."

"This is a fish," said Burl.

The Maestro's grip on the railing tightened. "It is something that is—*was*— alive."

Burl felt his insides cave in. His arm ached from holding up his prize. He lowered it to the sandy ground. Hung his head. The Maestro spoke again—quiet, distant.

"There is a basic problem here, Burl Crow. You seem to thrive on excitement. I'm quite dizzy with it."

He made his way down the steps, his hands thrust deep in his pockets. Burl watched him go, wavering like a drunk man down the beach. In his socks. His holey socks.

There were twenty-five kinds of pills in the medicine bag. Burl took them container by container and emptied them into the lake. He worked in a blind rage. His hands shook; his whole body shook.

The Maestro was well down the beach by then, sitting on a rock. He didn't see what was going on. Burl could take all day at it, and Nathaniel Gow would not notice. He couldn't see anything beyond his own nose. He didn't see the world or anyone in it except as it pleased him. He just made it up. Burl didn't exist. He was just someone to perform at, to play

< 7 2 >

games at. Burl had knocked on the door and got an ogre, not a wizard.

Twenty-five different drugs prescribed by several different doctors. Burl watched the capsules float on the water, then slowly dissolve. The pills sank. He saw the minnows nipping at them. He imagined them, puffy-faced and lethargic, prey to every predator in the lake.

He left all the containers lined up on the railing. But his display was rolling around on the deck before the Maestro found it, for the wind was blowing off the bay.

< 7 3 >

The Budd Car

BURL DIDN'T BOTHER to open the curtains. Best to sit in the dark, to curl up on the hard little bed the Maestro had made for him on the floor at the tail end of the piano. To wait for the door to fly open and his host, in a rage, to beat him with harsh and clever words.

The door did open, finally, but the slumped silhouette at the threshold was well beyond rage.

"Are you in here?"

Burl said nothing.

The Maestro entered carefully, as if he were a blind man feeling his way. This despite the fact that he crossed the room on a path of sunlight. He turned on the lamp at his bedside and, kneeling there, began to pack his clothes.

Burl moved; the floor squeaked. The Maestro looked up and into the corner where Burl sat watching him. With the

< 7 4 >

sunlight directly in his eyes, he could not sort out the boy from the shadows. But Burl could see his face clearly enough. The man looked defeated.

Into the emptiness of Burl's desolation, a new kind of strength coursed like poison. It stirred up something angry in him. A large anger on a barbed hook thrashing inside him, wanting out. He clenched his fists tight, felt the sharp message of his fingernails biting into the palms of his hands.

Without getting up, he reached out and flung the door closed. He tucked his angry fists in his armpits.

"I think it's time I was going," the Maestro said shakily. And he went back to packing, glancing up from time to time. After a while he started humming, but it was a nervous tune.

"The train comes through every other day at five," he said. "This just happens to be one of those other days."

Burl cleared his throat, uncertain what to do with his rage.

"I'm sorry," he shouted.

The Maestro shrugged.

"I told you," said Burl. "I don't know anything."

The Maestro raised an eyebrow. "You seem to have a treasure trove of talents particularly suited to living in the bush."

Burl's fingernails dug deeper into the flesh of his palms. "I was trying to help. I want to help."

The Maestro sighed wearily. "There was no chance—no real chance—I would be able to tolerate it out here for long. It was just a matter of time. I'll have to take my solitude in smaller doses, that's all."

"What about the things you said last night? About immortality. That stuff. About writing *The Revelation*."

The Maestro looked at him with surprise. "Amazing what nonsense a person says when he's just narrowly escaped being eaten by a bear."

The poisonous anger flared up in Burl. "It wasn't nonsense!"

< 7 5 >

The Maestro stopped packing, but he did not look Burl's way. "All right, since you insist. It wasn't nonsense. Let's just say I'm tired. Beaten. The wrestling match is over. Exit—ingloriously—the loser."

Burl got to his feet, leaned against the door. He noticed the Maestro watching him in sidelong glances, nervously.

"You're not leaving because of the bear. It's me," said Burl. "What about take two?"

The Maestro sat back on his heels, his hands pressing on his knees.

"From what point in time?" he said. "Where do we knock on that magical door and turn everything around?"

"From where I showed you the fish. How about that?"

"And how could we change things?"

"I would let it go. It would swim away."

"It wasn't the fish, Burl."

"The drugs. Can't we take-two the drugs?"

The man stared hard at him, fixed him with his eyes. Burl glared back.

"I believe," said the Maestro, "that you have as active an imagination as I do, Master Burl, but I fear neither of us can reconstitute my medication, no matter how much we might want to."

Burl abandoned the staring contest. "It was stupid of me. Stupid, stupid, stupid!"

"Please!" said the Maestro. "I loathe attention-getting displays unless I'm the one making them. Yes, it was stupid and thoughtless. However, you were provoked."

"I don't want you to go."

The Maestro stuffed another shirt into his suitcase. It was overflowing; it would never close.

"I only wanted to stay here one night."

< 7 6 >

"Nonsense. You are running away from some dreadful situation. You need a sanctuary. That's what cleaning the shed and catching the fish were all about. Unfortunately, the monks of the holy order of Nathaniel Gow are a solitary lot. We do not welcome strangers, even when, sorrowfully, they are refugee children."

He was busy trying to close his bulging suitcase.

"You can't go," said Burl. "Let me do for you. I'll stay out of your hair." It all came blurting out, dreams in the nearest shape that words could make of them. "I can sleep in the shed. There's room there, once I've got rid of the garbage. I'm happier outside, I'll—"

"You'll what? Catch me some more fish? What exactly will you do?" The Maestro sat on his suitcase, exhausted from the strain of trying to shut it and shut out Burl. He buried his head in his hands.

"I could take the train down to Presqueville and get your prescriptions filled out for you. I wouldn't steal the money. I'd be back right away."

The Maestro stood up and stared at Burl. "You are a remarkably persistent lad." He looked closely at him, as if seeing him for the first time. "You know, I *did* look like you. Your eyes are brown and mine blue, but our faces are not all that dissimilar. The same skinny chin, the same fire in the eyes." He seemed as if he might go on, as if there was a whole trunkful of memories he might spill out, but he caught himself. Then he turned his attention back to the problem of the suitcase. With his toe he opened it again. He began to lift things out. Burl watched hopefully, but soon it became apparent that the Maestro was only emptying out what did not fit. He closed the top again and snapped the locks.

< 7 7 >

✻　✻　✻

What happened next—the sequence of it—was hard for Burl to make clear in his head. Later when he tried, it was all a blur of confusion.

At some point the Maestro was leaving, draped in overcoats, scarf, hat, and gloves as if he were stepping into a February blizzard instead of a windy late-summer afternoon. He carried only his suitcase.

There was a path—an Indian trail as old as birch-bark canoes—that led from the lake to the train. The CPR twin-coach passenger service—the Budd car, as it was called locally—would pick him up sometime around five.

Were there good-byes? Did the Maestro tip his hat, wave?

And Burl? Had he actually stood at the door watching the man leave as if he were a departing houseguest? At what moment did it dawn on him that he had not merely been left behind—for that was the way he thought of it at the time—but that he had been left the cabin?

He could stay there. He had not been kicked out. The Maestro had just walked off as if for an afternoon stroll. Was that it, then? Would he be back?

Living with his father, Burl had learned not to want too much. He had learned to steal his pleasure. Now suddenly, and without ceremony, a dream seemed to have been dropped in his lap.

It was when he was looking around the cabin, daring to think of what he would do first, how he would make it his, that he noticed the worktable with the music on it. *The Book of Revelation*. At the foot of the chair lay the Maestro's scuffed brown-leather briefcase with straps that looked dog-chewed.

Burl rolled back the curtains, let the light flood in. He looked back at the table. How many pages? Hundreds, it seemed. He looked through one of the piles. On the left side of the score was listed beside each clef the instrument meant to play that line of music. How was it done? When the violin finished the first line, did the viola take over, then the cello and then the bass, one after the other?

He looked through a few pages. No, the bars were numbered. It must be that all these instruments played bar one together. But then how was it possible to hear what it sounded like when you were writing it down? How could anyone hear all these instruments in his head at once?

Burl sat down. He didn't understand much about music, but he grasped one extraordinary fact. It would take incredible concentration to write it. And in the same moment as he realized this, he also understood what the Maestro had been saying about his need for solitude. Now he was heading back to the Shadow. Now he would take his solitude in smaller doses. What did that mean? Weekend visits to the camp?

Burl gritted his teeth. No beating by Cal could have made him feel as terrible as he felt right then.

But it was that discovery that brought him to his senses. In a matter of a few minutes, he deposited all the music and notes and lists and the pencils, too—for perhaps they were special music-writing pencils—into the briefcase until it bulged and the straps strained. Then he tore out the door and up the path the Maestro had taken into the woods. That was the thing, later, that most mystified the boy about his own actions: he was giving the Maestro a second chance to come to his senses.

The way was steep, the load heavy. He imagined catching up to the Maestro and the man smacking his forehead. "My God, what was I thinking. Of course I can't let you stay there." As he trudged through the forest, Burl take-twoed this unwelcome scenario right out of his head.

< 7 9 >

"It's yours, Burl. It's no place for the likes of me." Burl savored the sound of that.

It was a half-hour walk to the track, and the path was far from smooth going. There was the odd tree down, and in places there was underbrush that needed cutting back. Burl ran, shifting the briefcase from hand to hand, sometimes hugging it to his chest with both arms. It was so heavy.

Skittering down the final steep hill that led to the tracks, he found himself gasping for breath. He had run most of the way.

Mile 29. There was a sign and a light, nothing more. The land fell off steeply on the other side of the track to the river.

The Maestro was balancing on the rail, his hands behind his back, humming. His shoddy suitcase sat on the black stone slag upon which the tracks ran. He turned and seemed surprised to see Burl there.

"Your music," said Burl, approaching him, his heart pounding like a locomotive in his chest.

The Maestro eyed the case strangely, as if it were some alien animal that might bite. He dug his hand into his pocket for a handkerchief and wiped Burl's face clean of sweat.

"Put the infernal bag down," he said. Obediently Burl lowered it, letting it lean against his feet. "This is the act of a contrite child."

"I know what I did was wrong," said Burl.

The Maestro crouched and felt one of the tattered straps of the briefcase. A smile broke out on his face. "A dog did this," he said. "His name was Pilgrim. He used to rest his snout on the keyboard sometimes when I was practicing. When I retired from the concert stage, I had this idea that I was going to build an animal shelter somewhere in the country and take in strays. Oh, it was never a real option, I suppose, but my intention was good. Then out of the blue drops this

< 8 0 >

stray boy—you—and do I extend even a crumb of hospitality? People are harder than animals, I guess." His eyes cleared. "I'll leave the music," he said, "until next time."

Burl picked up the briefcase. "So you'll be back?"

The Maestro looked up the track, looked at his watch. The train was already late. "Of course I shall come up again. There's the piano to see to. I'll have to do something about it before the winter. Like its master, it's sensitive to the cold."

There was only one thought on Burl's mind. It was now or never. He gathered up his courage. "If I could stay for a while, I'd make sure I left the place tidy and safe, like from bears and stuff."

"And you'd live on fish and berries, is that it? Make a bow and arrow and shoot yourself a moose?"

"I'd be okay. I wouldn't eat none—any—of your food."

The Maestro shook his head. "Nonsense. Help yourself. I may not have been able to cope with you as a houseguest, but I don't begrudge you whatever my meager larder can provide."

"Thank you," said Burl.

The Maestro looked at him, right into Burl's worried heart.

"You aren't likely to chop up the piano for kindling, are you?"

"I'll guard it with my life."

"And absolutely no cruising on the lake in it."

Burl smiled. "I promise."

Tentatively, the Maestro reached out and patted him on the shoulder.

Then a whistle blew. Burl knew what to do. He stepped out onto the track and flagged the Budd car down.

"When are you coming up again?" he asked.

Maybe it was the clanging of the approaching train, the dragonlike wheezing of the brakes, but the Maestro looked suddenly youthful with excitement.

< 8 1 >

"You mean how long can you stay?" He watched the train drawing to a clamorous stop. He handed up his bag to the man in the door of the freight section. Then he headed toward the passenger entrance farther down the length of the two dirty silver cars.

"I'll keep you posted," he said.

"How?"

The Maestro smiled. "Smoke signals, perhaps." He climbed up the steps. And if he said more, it was lost to Burl in the whine of the wheels, steel on steel, as the train started up again.

< 8 2 >

Alone

HE MADE A FIRE on the beach. He cut up the bass the way his father had shown him. There was no flour in the kitchen, so he ground up Arrowroot cookies—there were many boxes of them. He ground the cookies to a fine powder to coat the fillets. He found a can of small potatoes, a can of creamed corn.

He had sat on the slope by the railway track for some time after the Budd car had gone. Absently he had plucked at the long grass there, thinking, regaining strength for the walk back. In his exploration he had discovered that the hill was covered with wild licorice. He picked it and carried it back, and after supper he made licorice tea and watched the moon come up. With lots of honey it didn't taste half bad. He let the fire burn down to nothing, let the cold night air steal in on the

< 8 3 >

circle of warmth. Only when there was no warmth left did he go in.

The cabin was flooded with moonlight. He had turned off the generator as soon as he had returned from the track. He had no idea how much fuel was left, but he planned to use it sparingly. He hoped to stay for as long as he could. He lit a candle and carried it to the piano. He played the chords the Maestro had taught him. He tried to see how quietly he could play the passage. It was the part in *The Revelation* about the lamb opening something. A silence in heaven—something like that. He got up and carefully removed the music from the briefcase. He thumbed through the pages, but, although they were numbered, he had no way of knowing where the "Silence in Heaven" might be.

The Bible lay on the table. He flipped it open, flipped it to the end of the New Testament. There it was: the Book of Revelation.

He made the bed, pulled the sheets tight, smoothed out the blankets. Then he stripped and lay down naked between the covers, listening to the silence. He blew out the candle and tried to sleep, but his mind was too full. After a moment he got up and dug through his pockets for the key to the shed. He found a flashlight and, naked, stepped outside onto the deck. It was cold but still. He listened. Nothing grunted, nothing crashed through the brush. So he made his way through the woods to the shed. He opened the door and turned on the generator.

Back in the cabin, shivering, he curled up in bed, switched on the bedside lamp, and opened the Bible to the last book. Until then he had never really thought of the Bible having an end. It seemed so large. But here it was: a crazy vision of the ending of everything. The Book of Revelation wasn't long, but he found it hard to read and skipped chunks of it, depending on

< 8 4 >

the titles and subtitles to get the gist of the story. There were footnotes, but they didn't help a lot. He might read them later, though. Suddenly there seemed time to do that.

The lamb was a pretty strange creature, with seven horns and seven eyes. There was a scroll with seven seals on it, and no one could open it to see what God had written there. No one except the lamb. He tried to imagine a lamb opening a letter. It was the kind of thing that could only happen in a dream.

After the silence in heaven was when things really started to happen. Fire and blood and more fire. And every terrible thing that happened started with a trumpet sounding. There were seven trumpets altogether. Everything was seven in the Book of Revelation.

He thought about that a bit—the Bible heavy on his lap, his head growing heavier on his pillow. The wind picked up outside. He heard the water lapping against the posts of the deck. He plumped the book down on the floor, switched off the light, and fell way down into the kindest sleep he had ever known.

It rained that night. The rain unlocked him.

< 8 5 >

Bea

THE DE HAVILLAND BEAVER seemed to tumble out of the sky, skimming down the hills behind the cabin and landing on the lake off the north shore. Burl watched it from the beach, saw it turn its orange nose toward him and motor in. It was late in the afternoon. He had been bathing in the lake and had changed into one of the shirts the Maestro had left behind, a white dress shirt. The tails were out; the large shirt billowed in the wind. He had the sleeves rolled up high.

He had heard the floatplane coming, seen it circle the lake, flying low, then disappear out of sight behind the ridge and out of hearing, only to reappear moments later, making an approach into the onshore wind. Burl had been in the cabin for four days, and this was his first sign of civilization.

Shielding his eyes from the sun, he could see there was only the pilot on board. He tried to imagine his father crouching

< 8 6 >

in the hold, ready to leap out once the plane reached the shore. This fantasy somehow failed to arouse any real sense of panic.

The provincial police operated planes; there was no other way of getting around in the north in a hurry. But there were no police markings on this plane. And as it drew nearer to shore, Burl realized he wasn't going to run, whoever it was.

The racket of the engine drowned out the birdsongs. Then, just offshore, the engine was cut, and the plane drifted in until its pontoons nosed up onto the beach. The pilot climbed out of the cockpit, down the ladder to the pontoon. A woman.

She gave Burl a businesslike nod, took off her mirror shades, and twisted to get a kink out of her back.

"Rabbits and hares," she said loudly, as if the motor were still running.

She jumped ashore. Got a soaker but didn't seem to mind. "You Burl?" she asked. He nodded. "Bea Clifford," she said. "Skookum Airways." She shook his hand.

Seeing he was barefooted, she directed him to a cleat at the rear end of the pontoon. He waded out, grabbed ahold of it, and helped swing the plane around so that the tail was facing the beach. The pontoons were tapered toward the back, and together he and Bea dragged the plane up the shore a bit. Bea had a long rope that she tied in a clove hitch to the cleat. She tethered the plane to a large driftwood log.

"Onshore breeze," she said. "Plane's not going anywhere fast."

When Burl still did not reply, she pretended to knock on his forehead. Anybody home? Burl backed off.

"It's September first, kid. You've always got to say 'Rabbits and hares' the first of the month. Not that I'm superstitious."

She put her hands on her hips, gave Burl a quick but intense once-over. Then she surveyed the spot. "Great camp, eh?"

Burl forced himself to say yes.

"Shed's up that way, as I recall," she said. Then she jumped back aboard the pontoon, opened the door. "Come on, fellah. I'm gonna need a little help with this."

Burl waded out. "Mr. Gow isn't here anymore," he said.

Bea hefted a cardboard box out of the cab. She balanced it with her knee while she checked her watch. "I got a party wants out of Pogamasing at six, so put a little hustle into it, eh?"

The box was heavy with groceries.

"There must be some mistake," he said.

"That might be true," said Bea. "But it's not my mistake."

Burl took the carton, which he left on the shore. When he returned, she was reaching into the breast pocket of her flight jacket. She showed him an invoice. "North End Ghost Lake. Old Starlight Claim. Round Trip. Burl."

"That's all I got written here," she said. "Mr. Gow gave me the shopping list when he passed through a few days back, but what with people closing up summer lodges and resorts and such, I couldn't free up one of the boys until yesterday."

She inspected him again. "You don't look like you've been suffering too much."

In a bit of a daze, Burl lugged a second box of groceries to the shore. Five more boxes followed in rapid succession, heavy with cans and stacked high with packaged goods: noodles, rice, tea, coffee, cookies, bread, and canned milk.

"Oo-ee," said Bea. She had stopped to admire a line of fish Burl had secured to the underside of the deck so that they could swim in the shallows. He had caught them that morning—four bass and a couple of perch. The bass were a good size, plenty for supper and breakfast, too.

"Good fishin' here?" she asked. She stopped and took a good long gander at the lake. She breathed in deeply. "Very pretty. Very pretty."

< 8 8 >

not claim his complete attention. "Burl," it read. Not "Burl Crow," as he had feared. By now there might be a search party out looking for him. That is, if anybody had declared him missing.

He glanced at Bea. She was helping herself to a good long look at him. He wondered if she knew who he was.

"Anything wrong?" asked Bea.

"No," said Burl. Then, with a shock, he noticed the price of the flight, over three hundred dollars. The invoice was stamped PAID.

Bea was busy unhitching the Beaver from its mooring.

There was one other thing on Burl's mind.

"What does it mean, 'Round Trip'?"

Bea leaned on one of the wing struts. "Well, Burl. As pretty a spot as you got here, I hadn't planned on staying. So you see, it's a round trip you pay for."

Burl made one last inspection of the invoice and then handed it back.

"You can send anything back you want. The trip's paid for. Anything up to twelve hundred pounds. Yourself included."

There was nothing Burl wanted to send back.

"You sure now?" she said.

"Nothing," he said. "Thank you."

She looked out at the lake again, my-my-mying quietly to herself. "You got yourself one honey of a retreat here." There was a directness to the statement that annoyed Burl, though he couldn't say why. She was right.

"You known him long?" she asked.

Burl was on his guard. "What did he say?"

"He said he had a young sentinel and custodian—those were the words he used—watching over things for him till he could get up again. Did he hire you?"

Again Burl didn't answer.

< 9 0 >

The next part of the load was heavy. A forty-fi
drum of diesel fuel. The two of them improvised a
boards Burl hauled out from under the cabin. Once
the drum on the beach, Bea was winded.

Burl headed to the house for something to drink. He
her back a canned cola and one for himself. He
saving them; he was down to three. Now, it seemed
another three dozen.

Bea took a good long pull on the can. "Caught
guard," she said. "Sure I did." She laughed. What
Right from her boots. "Jeez," she said, handing him
empty cola can. "There's something else." She clam
into the cockpit and backed out of the plane carryi
and reel and a brown paper bag.

"Barry picked you up a coupla things: some line
hooks, and stuff. A coupla lures: a Hula Popper, a
Wobbler—hell, I never caught anything but bottom
of those. But then Barry doesn't know his butt from
sandwich, most days."

Burl pulled the plastic package from the bag. The
gleamed gold.

"Thanks," he said. It seemed a lame thing to say.
he hadn't spoken much lately. "Was the rod Mr. Gov

She looked at him inquisitively, looked at the N
his shirt. He felt his hand floating up to cover the m

"Mr. Gow? Is that what you call him?"

Burl didn't quite like the look on her face. He didn'

"Yeah. Yeah," said Bea, good-natured again. "It
idea."

"Can I see that paper?" Burl asked. Bea handed
invoice. Ghost Lake. He had not known this plac
name until then. The Old Starlight Claim. That mu:
prospector the Maestro had mentioned. But these th

< 8 9 >

"No," said Bea. "Somehow I didn't think so." She gave him one more penetrating inspection, then put on her shades. "Well, we'll be seeing you again, Burl, I imagine."

"Yes," he said. "Thanks again for the stuff."

"Don't thank me."

She unhitched the plane and pushed it back into the water. The waves pushed at the Beaver, rocking it like a rocking horse. Bea climbed back on board. Burl retreated a little up the beach. Bea flipped down her window, waved.

"You take care now," she said, her face up near the tiny opening.

Burl nodded. Then he waded out so he could see her just as she was closing the window.

"Tell Mr. Gow thank you for me," he said.

She smiled. "I'll be sure to send Mr. Gow your regards."

Then the silence of Ghost Lake was shattered for the second time in less than an hour as the plane roared off.

Burdened with both gratitude and curiosity, Burl began to heft the groceries up to the cabin. There was easily a month's worth of supplies.

< 9 I >

The Cabin on the Cliff

HE ATE, SLEPT, FISHED, explored, flattened cans, played on the piano, counted shooting stars, tried reading the Bible, unearthed a flint arrowhead, conducted the northern lights, watched the poplars turn yellow, built a raft out of planks and plywood, wrote his name in frost on the railing of the deck, tried to remember what his father looked like, his mother, washed his clothes and hung them out to dry in the north wind, made roaring bonfires on the beach with fat pine, resinous and hot.

Alone, Burl found himself caught between anticipation and relief. But he got on in fine style with the business of living. The Maestro would return when he returned. And when he did, Burl was determined not to get in his way. To that end, he started work, making something of a sleeping quarter in the shed.

< 9 2 >

It was a challenge. There were all kinds of building material—rigid insulation, lengths of two-by-four, oddly shaped scraps of plywood—but after he'd made his raft, there was not enough of anything to actually wall off the diesel engine.

Then one day, while he was working in the shed, his mind wandered to what he had read on the invoice. The Old Starlight Claim. Burl stopped what he was doing. Maybe the prospector had never found gold or whatever he was looking for, but he might have made himself a cabin of some kind. He stepped outside the shed and was surprised that it had never occurred to him before to look. For right outside the door, the path that led up from the beach continued right past the shed, if only he'd had eyes to see. It was well and truly overgrown.

There are paths in the woods. Tunnels. They still have walls if you can make your eyes adjust, see the signs. The hill climbed steeply. Branches brushed against Burl's face, closed in on him. He kept his eyes peeled. Finally he found a blaze in a tree trunk. He went on. Then he found another blaze, long healed but still a sign. He was high enough to catch glimpses of the lake through the poplars. Then he was on a rocky ridge. He came to a digging site—not a mine, but a man-made depression in the ground. And then, finally, he came upon what he had hoped for. A tiny, perfect cabin not much bigger than the Maestro's shed.

The door bristled with sharp black spikes, business side out. The windows were shuttered in the same manner. This was bear-proofing at its gruesome best! For all that, the door was not locked. In fact, when the latch was opened, the spiked door swung out to reveal a plain wooden door behind it. Burl ventured inside.

There was an iron bedstead. A wide shelf under the window near the door with a large white enameled bowl, a couple of tin saucepans, a black iron frying pan. On a narrow shelf above

< 9 3 >

this counter, beside the window, sat a couple of plates, bowls, cups, and a wooden box with a few pieces of cutlery in it neatly wrapped in a tea towel. There was a tin box with matches inside. In the corner sat a tiny old woodstove vented through the wall. A cast-iron teapot sat on the top. That was all. There was no closet—only three hooks on the wall. There was no chest of drawers but only another shelf near the door, empty. There was a layer of dust on everything, several dead flies, mouse droppings. But otherwise the place was as neat as a pin.

Burl walked around the little cabin again and again, marveling at its orderliness. Outside there was a neat stack of firewood with a sheet of plywood over it held down by rocks to keep it dry. Within half an hour of arriving at this spot, a person could have it cleaned up and a pot of tea bubbling on the stove.

On the south side of the building there was a bare and rocky outcropping from which Ghost Lake, almost the whole expanse of it, could be seen—all but the beach directly below where the pyramid stood.

Burl could not believe his luck. This is where he would stay when the Maestro came back. He didn't need much. He could stay out of the Maestro's way when he was composing or when he was in one of his moods. He would come down to cook meals and fix stuff that needed fixing. He would earn his keep. It was all so perfect.

Burl closed up the cabin carefully. On the way back down the hill, he freshened up the blazes on the trees and added a couple of new ones. He would clear some of this trail. It would be something to do with his time. He had lots of time.

He was far too busy for loneliness to enter his mind. It was September, and he could not remember a September when he wasn't at school. He thought about Mrs. Agnew. He imagined showing her around the cabin, making her supper there.

He thought about her finding the book she had given him, in his old desk. He hoped she wouldn't think he hadn't wanted it. Nothing could have been further from the truth.

< 9 5 >

Swept Away

A MONTH PASSED. A month and a bit. Burl measured the days in groceries. His boxes emptied slowly but steadily.

Fall set in hard. It rained in cold gray sheets, and when it wasn't raining there was invariably a cloud cover that hung like a badly strung and leaky tarp over Ghost Lake. On bad days Burl stayed in and fought his way through Revelation.

Flickering lights didn't make it easy. There was something wrong with the generator: a dirty filter, contaminated fuel— he wasn't sure what. He wasn't sure which he'd run out of first: food or electricity.

It was hunting season. Flights in and out of the bush increased until there were planes coming Burl's way almost daily, but none of them touched down on his lake. Each distant buzzing brought on a low-level pain in Burl's head, like a tooth that needed attending.

< 9 6 >

He couldn't be sure the Maestro would allow him to stay. He was not a boy who had grown up with any guarantees about anything, but this—this he wanted so much. He imagined scene upon scene with Nathaniel Orlando Gow. He prepared himself for every kind of take two.

Nothing, however, quite prepared him for what was to happen.

Indian summer rolled in. And so it was on a rare sunny day that Bea returned. Burl was out on his raft fishing for pickerel in deep water off the cliff from which he had first spied Ghost Lake. Despite the sun, a metallic, wintry-tasting cold came up from the bottom of the lake. His feet were frozen up to the ankles; buoyancy was not his craft's best quality. Then came the drone and the speck in the wide sky, getting closer.

He recognized the orange floatplane with the black stripe down the side. He waved. Bea tipped her wing at him. She did not need to circle upland to make her approach, for even on a fine day now the wind blew nearly always out of the north.

He rowed hard, but with a piece of one-by-three whittled into a very rough paddle, his progress was slow. Bea reached the beach before he did. He looked to shore expectantly. She didn't seem to have a cargo or a passenger this time around. She stood on the beach kicking at the sand with her toe, her hands in the back pockets of her jeans.

Burl straightened up. He stopped rowing. Something about her stance made him want to just let the offshore breeze blow him away down the lake.

She gazed out at him. She still had her shades on, but she held him in her vision as surely as if he were a runway on a stormy day. So he paddled again, despite the wind and despite the churning in his stomach. She was reeling him in.

Bea gave him a hand to haul his raft onto the shore. When

< 9 7 >

he looked up to thank her, the words stuck in his throat. The set of her jaw was grim.

"I got some bad news," she said.

Once upon a time, Burl's mother told Cal to show the boy a little love. So Cal had written the letters L O V E with a ballpoint pen on the knuckles of his fist and asked Burl how much love he wanted. Nothing bad ever really came as a surprise to Burl.

"It's your Mr. Gow," said Bea, clearing her throat a bit. "There isn't any easy way to say this. He's gone. He died."

Burl took a couple of deep breaths, as if he were going to dive for something a long way down.

"It was a coupla days back. I got up here as soon as I could."

Burl held on to his breath, wouldn't let it escape.

"It was in all the papers," said Bea. "Front page in the *Toronto Star*." She seemed surprised that Gow demanded so much attention. "Even the *Sudbury Star*. I got them here. Thought you might like to see."

She didn't wait for an answer. She brought him the papers from the cockpit. There was a picture of an intense young man hunched over the keyboard of a piano. Burl's eyes scanned the story: "One of the world's great pianists ... massive stroke ... eccentric genius ... recluse ... the music world mourns ..."

He looked up. Bea was staring at him expectantly. He wondered if she was waiting for him to cry. He became aware of how cold his feet were. He sat on a rock and took off his shoes, his soaking socks.

She showed him the other paper. The face of the pianist here was older, more haggard.

"He booked a flight for the middle of this month," said Bea, stowing her shades away in her pocket. "Not for him," she said. "Wild horses wouldn't get him up in a plane." She

< 9 8 >

laughed a little at this, as if nothing could be quite so incomprehensible to her as someone with a fear of flying. "You okay, kid?"

"Pardon?"

"He say anything to you about his plans?"

Burl swallowed hard. "Just that he was coming."

"So what happens now?" she said.

Burl stared at his feet. Couldn't speak.

"He paid for the trip already. Normally, folks pay the day they fly, but he was pretty determined."

Burl took another couple of deep breaths. Whatever he was diving for was buried way deep in the lake, in the mud somewhere a long way down. It was cold down there.

"He was firm about payin' for the flight in advance." Bea seemed uncomfortable. "I tried to tell him there was no need, but he wouldn't listen. When I heard he died, I found myself thinkin', maybe he had a premonition. Know what I mean?"

Burl looked at her. "He knew he was going to die?"

"That's what I figure."

"Then why would he want to pay you for the trip?"

Bea shrugged. "I thought maybe you'd be able to help me with that one."

Burl pushed his hair out of his eyes. It was almost two months long. His mind was racing. "For supplies, I guess."

Bea sniffed in a matter-of-fact kind of way. "Give me a little help here, Burl." She didn't snap at him, but the words were peppery. "I have no instructions. One round trip, all paid for. That's all I know. Do I have to spell this out for you?"

Burl cleared his throat. "I don't want out," he said. "I mean ... thanks, but I have to stay."

Bea crossed her arms, didn't move. She looked out over the lake. "You got money for the Budd then?"

< 9 9 >

He didn't answer. She seemed to know the truth of his situation.

Bea licked her finger and held it up. "Oo-ee, that nor'wester is freshening for sure. Nice enough now, but I'd be willing to bet that's winter coming."

Burl glanced at her through his bangs.

"You're not a city kid, are you?"

Burl knew he had to say something. She wasn't going to leave him alone. He shook his head.

"You didn't come up with him," she said.

"No."

"So he found you here? You were squattin' in the cabin?"

Burl shook his head. "I knew he was here. I was looking for him."

Burl could feel her eyes on him. "And he was lookin' for you?"

Burl nodded. "Yeah, he was looking for me. He was kind of expecting me."

He glanced at her. When he said no more, she frowned. Then she looked at her watch.

"Well, if you're from around these parts, you know something about winter. And I know firsthand what supplies you've got."

Burl hung his head.

"What do you say, Burl? Was he coming up himself? Was he taking you back down south with him? Or did he have some plans to winterize this place?"

There was a lump in Burl's throat. It was as if she was rooting around in his dreams. Suddenly, for the first time in a month, he was very lonely.

Her face softened a bit. "Burl. It's none of my beeswax, but I'd suggest you get back to what folks you've got."

"There's no one else."

<1 0 0>

Bea leaned her foot on the cleat of the pontoon. The water lapped and slapped at the sand. Some gulls shrieked.

"Looks like you've been doing some cleaning up around here."

Burl followed her eyes. There had been enough stain left to slap another coat on the deck. He was surprised she had noticed.

"Burl," she said. "You seem like a resourceful kid. But you know as well as I do that you can't live through the winter in an uninsulated cabin. I was the one brought in that Delco generator. A fine machine, but unless you've found your own little cache of diesel fuel, you're toast, kiddo. Yesterday's toast."

Burl felt a frantic wave rising in him. "I was supposed to be staying here," he said. "I can't just leave."

"Well, I've got a few minutes. . . ."

"No!" He looked back toward the cabin longingly. His cabin. "The piano," he said. "It can't take the cold. I can't just leave it."

Bea raised her eyebrows. "Well, if you can find some way to fold it up small . . ." But she wasn't in a joking mood. "Burl, let's get real. You can come back here. Right? But for now, you don't have a lot of choices."

He could come back. Burl grabbed on to that idea tightly. "I can't go without shutting the place down proper."

"Okay," said Bea, rubbing her hands together. "Now you're talking sense."

Burl looked at her. "There's fitted shutters for the windows. I found them under the cabin. Bear protection."

She nodded.

"I've got to clean the place up. I've got to leave it just right. I've got to pack and clean and—"

"Burl!" She raised her voice, cutting him off. "It's time to fish or cut bait. You know what I mean?"

Burl was shaking. The whole beautiful thing was collapsing in on him.

"Wake up, kiddo," she said. Her voice was firm. "This must be pretty scary, losing him like this. But you've gotta make some decisions, here and now."

He looked at her straight on.

"I've got as long as you need," she said. "But my schedule is way too full for emotional breakdowns. I failed nursemaid school. And I can't come flying in here to see how you're doing. I've got a business to run."

She let this sink in. "Now, I've got some camps of my own," she said. "So I sure appreciate what you're saying about shutting the place up all shipshape and Bristol fashion."

Burl was looking at the cabin. He knew how little food he had left. His only alternative to flying out with Bea was to walk out. Along the tracks it was twenty-nine miles to Presque-ville. And that walk took him through Pharaoh.

"Burl," said Bea. "It's either now or *dak jim*."

Burl chose now. Bea helped. Though the churchlike windows were high and there were four shutters per window, there was a twenty-foot aluminum ladder, and the work went fast enough.

The faulty generator needed shutting down; the last of the garbage was gathered, the perishables boxed up.

The cabin was as clean as a whistle. There was next to nothing to pack. He had come with nothing, and he would leave that way. Almost. He packed the few clothes the Maestro had left behind in a brown paper bag. His own clothes hardly fit him anymore.

When Bea wasn't looking, when she had gone back down to start up the plane, he played the opening chords of the "Silence in Heaven" one last time, quietly as could be.

"I'll be back," he whispered to the piano, though he had no idea when or how. Then Bea called his name. She sounded

<102>

as if she was losing her patience. Quickly, Burl took all the sheets and blankets off the bed and some fishing line and wrapped up the piano as snugly as he could.

Then he found himself climbing into a bush plane for the first time in his life. He felt like someone evacuated from a place under siege, a village in the path of a forest fire.

Liftoff. Burl looked down and took in the shape of Ghost Lake. He committed the shape to memory. He would find it again through any wilderness; out of any sky he would pick it out from all the million other lakes.

The Beaver shook and rattled in the crosswinds; climbed and leveled off and dropped again as it beat a course south. Burl was swept away by the thrill of the ride.

"Dak jim," he said, shouting above the engine's roar. "What is that?"

"Korean stew," yelled Bea. "I flew in a war over there, sonny. Lied about my age. Lied about my sex. Lied my way right into a war."

Suddenly the plane fell again, and Burl gasped. The wind thumped them down the hard blue steps of the sky.

Bea laughed, pulled up her wing tips. "Hell's bells, kid. I've flown through worse crap than this."

She looked steadily at him, and when he returned her gaze, all he could see was himself two-faced—mirrored in her glasses.

"Who are you, Burl?"

He knew what he wanted to tell her. What she expected him to say. What she'd been trying to pry out of him from the start.

"I'm his son," he said.

< 1 0 3 >

PART TWO

Natalie Agnew

NATALIE AGNEW STOOPED to pick up a discarded soda can. The empty was frosty cold with dew. There was another one down by the water's edge. She slid down the bank to recover it and then squatted there to watch the river.

The Skat was far from picturesque. Not brown, really, she thought, but rust-colored, like so much else about this part of the world: the rocks, the cars and pickups. From this angle she could see where the sunlight filtered down through the ties on the railway bridge overhead, laying bands of gold on the river. Like a xylophone, she thought.

She and David had driven up to Pharaoh from Presqueville early that morning. He was a social planner, a consultant to the native council at the Leather Belt Reservation. He had a meeting and she had come along for the ride to see the fall colors, to get out of Presqueville, to be with him. But there wasn't really much in the way of fall color—no maples, at least. She got that hungry feeling for the Eastern Townships, where she had grown up. She could almost taste the maple syrup.

She had walked through what there was of Pharaoh and was now at the end of the road that served the town as main street, though she had seen no sign to suggest it had a name. David had said, "It would take some inspiration to actually name a street." David wasn't keen on Pharaoh.

"Yes, but somebody named the place Pharaoh," she had said. "And that took a *lot* of imagination."

The road ended abruptly, petered out to a sandy path, then bush and litter. She was thinking of going back to the car to see if there was a garbage bag in the trunk. She thought of David laughing at her—Natalie the garbage crusader. That convinced her it was worth the walk. It was good to hear his big healthy laugh. But she would wait a minute, sit on a rock and watch the xylophone shifting tunelessly with every breeze.

It was Saturday. She would take the time to enjoy watching the dew melt as the October sun rose out of the bush. She wasn't from these parts. She kept calling it the forest, but bit by bit the locals were convincing her that it was nothing so lofty. It was bush, plain and simple.

She would sit and count what passed before her eyes down the Skat: an oak leaf redder even than the river, a spray of yellow poplar. Sure there were fall colors; you just had to look.

Pharaoh. Burl Crow came from here. She stood and looked back down the road as if thinking of him might make him materialize. The road was still empty.

The first day of term, Sherri Kelso had come up to her with *The Red Fairy Book*. She had found it tucked into the back of her desk. Somehow Natalie hadn't been surprised. Boys that

<106>

age were hard critters to figure out. Leaving her present behind could mean anything, or nothing at all.

But she was a little sad, when she thought about it, that Burl hadn't dropped around to visit. Mind you, how would he? He was a long way from Presqueville, and the bus from the high school in Vaillancourt probably took all of what was left of after-school. It had been unreasonable to expect to see him again.

She considered Burl. He was intelligent, imaginative, but he held it in check. Not slyly, like an ace up the sleeve. More as though he were carrying an egg through the playground at recess, never knowing where the next jolt might come from. She had noticed angry bruises on him. And a hunger in his eyes.

He was full of promise, she thought. Absently Natalie made a circle out of stones on the riverbank. Full of promise. What a strange expression. As if life was a lie on the outside, but there was some other truth within. Was that Burl Crow?

She plopped a pebble in the water, watched her golden xylophone break into pieces.

She thought of Burl at Vaillancourt. How far some country kids had to go to get an education. No wonder so many of them gave up. It didn't seem fair. But what was? She wondered which teachers had gotten Burl. She hoped someone would be able to prod him along without scaring him.

She got to her feet, dusted off her hands. She had an idea. Why should she have expected Burl to reach her? She would reach him.

Yes. She would phone the high school and see how Burl was doing. First thing Monday.

<107>

Skookum Airways

IT WAS TWENTY-FIVE MILES as the crow flies from Pharaoh to the town of Intervalle, where the Skat emptied through a series of rapids into Bearberry Lake. Burl took to walking up to the rapids during his time off, to squat by the rushing waters. As he hunkered down on the cold rock, his senses filling up with the noise and sulfurous smell, there was a quiet place inside him he could escape to.

He didn't get much time off, but then he didn't really want it. He wanted money. Bea had hired him on part-time at Skookum. He was getting minimum wage, and he knew what he was going to do with every penny.

Bea had seen him work up at the cabin that last day at Ghost Lake. She had noticed how tidy the camp was, inside and out. He was quick, steady on the ladder, fussy. Once the shutters were on, he had gone around tightening the fasteners

<108>

with an improvised screwdriver. And when they were ready to leave, he had gone back to the cabin for one last check. She liked that. She told him so when she offered him the work. He wasn't in a position to say no. He had nowhere to go and no money. He had told Bea he was sixteen. He didn't think she believed him, but she didn't question it. He was paid under the table. There was no record of him working for Skookum. That suited his needs. It suited Bea's needs, too.

Duck-hunting season was in full swing, and there was lots of work around. Skookum was flying hunting parties from all over the province and the northern states into the bush. The company ran two planes and a helicopter. Bea leased six camp-sites on lakes throughout the Sudbury district. This time of the year she kept them filled pretty well weekly.

Burl helped load up. Everything had to be weighed: the packs and guns and cases of beer. There was a shack Bea called Cape Canaveral. It was head office, departure lounge, and staff room combined. Burl kept it tidy and served passengers coffee. He raked the scrap of lawn out front and ran errands. Bea kept him busy.

Skookum Airways was situated on a peninsula curving out like an apostrophe linking Intervalle Bay to the greater body of Bearberry Lake. There were no airstrips. The Beaver and the twin-engine Beechcraft took off from the lake; the chopper from a fenced helipad paved with asphalt, buckled by frost. Weeds grew through the cracks. There was a gravel parking lot, a Quonset hut machine shop, and, a short way off through the trees at the curling tip of the apostrophe, Bea's white clapboard bungalow.

The chopper pilot was called Harvey. Burl never learned his last name, hardly ever saw him. It was his twin-rotor Sikorsky that had carried the Maestro's grand piano into Ghost Lake.

<109>

A man named Palmateer owned and flew the Beechcraft. Burl never learned his *first* name. There were two other boys, Barry and Dieter. They were older than Burl—he wasn't sure how much. Dieter was training to fly. Harvey drove Dieter in every morning from town. Barry had some kind of mental problem. He shared the little house with Bea and Palmateer. Burl couldn't figure out if the three of them were related—if Bea and Palmateer were married, maybe; if Barry was their son. They didn't act like a family, but then Burl didn't have much experience with how families worked.

Dieter tended to be snooty with Barry. He teased him and invited Burl to join in on the fun. When Burl didn't, Dieter started being snooty with him as well and bossy, too, but not when Palmateer was around. Dieter was getting his license and then he was "outahere." He said that so much the phrase had fused into one word.

Burl saw more of Palmateer than of Bea. When he wasn't flying, Palmateer was always around the yard, either in the shop fixing something or in the office having a coffee. When Bea wasn't flying, she was often away, dressed up in heels and a suit, what Barry called her spook 'em clothes.

Palmateer and Harvey owned their own aircraft, but there was no question who ran Skookum Airways. It was Bea's operation. She was the one who made the business decisions, the glue that held the place together.

Burl slept in Cape Canaveral. There was a couch there and, in the staff room, a hot plate, fridge, and sink. He tagged along shopping with Palmateer and Barry and bought his own food and stuff in town.

Living in the office, he had to be up early and tidy everything up. The couch sat under a stuffed moose head wearing a

< I I 0 >

World War I air-ace helmet and goggles. Someone had draped the antlers with tinsel at a Christmas party sometime, and the decoration had become a fixture. There were maps and regulations on the walls and cartoons and bits and pieces of happy-customer memorabilia that made the place look cozy or a mess, depending on your point of view. To Burl it was a mess. He cleaned it up as best he could.

The couch was old and lumpy. Burl didn't sleep well. The porch light was always on, and there was a yard light as well. The road that led to Intervalle passed nearby, and, as small as the town was, there seemed to be traffic at the oddest hours. Burl wasn't used to the noise. But worse than that was the fact of the road itself. He was reconnected with civilization. The Intervalle Road led out to Highway 17, the Trans-Canada, and thirty miles west was the turnoff to Presqueville, from which a long dirt road led straight to Cal. Burl truly doubted that the Turd-mobile could get this far, but often he woke up sweating to the sound of a sputtering muffler and ran to the window, expecting to see a '63 Plymouth rolling into the yard. Then he would return to his bed and lie there, feeling every lump the ancient couch had to offer.

The first snow came and went. It wouldn't come for keeps for another month or so, but there would not likely be another warm spell. The second day Burl was there, Bea sent him off to Bélanger's in Intervalle for some winter gear. She advanced him enough pay to buy some clothes. He bought a duffel bag to carry it all in. She made him buy a toothbrush and a hairbrush as well. He had to look his best.

Burl laid his head on his hands. He had been there over a week and he had no idea what he was going to do next. Deer-hunting season in the Sudbury district would be coming up

<I I I>

late in October this year, and there was going to be a big harvest. That meant lots of hunters and lots of work. And then in November it would be moose season. He could probably stay right through to Christmas. And then . . .

Burl clambered out of bed and found his duffel bag. From one of the pockets he drew the only thing he had taken from the cabin, the letter to Nathaniel Gow—"Nog"—from Reggie Corngold. He returned to his makeshift bed and read it again. He lay there with the letter in his hands. Fell asleep like that.

On a blustery Thursday, his third week there, a party of four bowhunters arrived at the airport, having killed a couple of hours at the local bar waiting for their flight.

"Killed a few too many brain cells while they were at it," said Palmateer as he loaded the Beechcraft.

The hunters were dressed head to foot in camouflage, as if the hunt were already on. They were after bear. There was snow in the air, and they kept themselves warm by teasing Barry. They poked him a couple of times. "Hope we bag one this size," said one of them.

"Try your fawn bleat on him, Blake," said another. Blake made a whimpery little sound into Barry's ear as the boy loaded stuff on the weigh scales. The men roared with laughter and slapped their legs. Barry carried the stuff on down to the water's edge where the plane was tethered. He just shut himself off when that kind of thing happened. Burl had seen him do it before. Burl, on the other hand, was writhing inside. He couldn't stand to even look at the hunters.

"Now that fawn bleat usually attracts your smarter bears," said one of the men. "Better try something simple."

"How about I piss around the bait like a raccoon," said Blake, making as if to undo his fly. The hunters found this hilarious.

<I I 2>

"You get a raccoon pissing around your bait and you're gonna get bear big-time."

Burl was hauling a heavy box down to the plane. Palmateer must have seen the anger in his face. He spoke right up close to Burl.

"Picture this," he said. "Tonight while Barry is sleeping in his comfortable bed, those idiots are gonna be perched in a tree above a big trap smeared with smelly fish, freezing their useless butts off. So who's the stupid one, eh?"

Burl exploded in laughter. The hunters stopped talking. Turned to look.

"What's so friggin' funny, brown-face?"

One of the men sauntered down toward the loading dock, one called Gord. He stood in Burl's path. Head down, not wanting trouble, Burl made to pass him by. Gord stepped in front of him again. Burl looked up; he had no choice. Gord's sour and scornful expression changed. Burl could see him searching for something to say in his drunken brain, but before he could speak, Palmateer was out of the plane.

"Look, you fellahs," he said. "You keep holding up my boys, and the lake'll freeze over before we get you out to Onaping."

He said it mildly but with an authority that was hard to deny. Gord backed off with a big groveling kind of bow, which started his friends up again. The four of them moved off a few paces to light up another smoke. Blake found a can of beer in his pocket, cracked it open.

Palmateer sent Burl back to the shack for some more barf bags. "Maybe some bear'll get lucky," he said, winking.

But the confrontation had startled Burl, started him to shaking. He slipped on an icy patch and almost fell. Barry caught him.

"Don't let 'em ride you," said Barry.

< 1 1 3 >

It wasn't that. Burl had recognized Gord. Gord was one of his father's cronies. And he was pretty sure Gord had recognized him. When he returned from the shack, he dared to look over at the four men. Through a haze of cigarette smoke and frozen breath, Gord was looking his way.

< I I 4 >

The Love Child

THERE WAS A MAP in the office behind the counter. A series of maps of northern Ontario, all joined together. There were circles drawn on it radiating out from Skookum Airways. Each line represented a new price zone. Burl had looked at the map often since he arrived. Ghost Lake was there. It wasn't named, but he knew the shape of it.

There was a square dot representing the tiny cabin on the cliff. Nothing for the Maestro's pyramid.

With a finger Burl traced the path of his journey through the bush that day in late August when he had left his father behind by the riverbank. And he traced the helicopter route of the piano from Skookum Airways directly to Ghost Lake. He found the point where the piano had crossed the Skat. With his finger he followed the hairline that was the River Skat all the way down to Intervalle.

<115>

The night of the bowhunters, Burl marked in the Maestro's cabin on the north shore. He stared at the map for a long time. Long enough to start taking down the shutters in his mind, air the place out. He couldn't stay at Skookum. Gord had recognized him. He was hunting now, but when he got back he would tell Cal. Burl was sure of it.

But it wasn't just Gord that was on his mind. He was worried about the piano. He had promised the Maestro he would take care of things.

The piano. How he missed his few chords, the "Silence in Heaven." How hard could it be to learn more? He wanted more, though now who could teach him?

He had stopped at the hardware store in Intervalle a few days earlier and talked with a guy there about woodstoves. He had thought about trying to get the little woodstove down from the miner's cabin, but the task seemed almost impossible. Getting a woodstove to the cabin would be hard however he went about it—unless, maybe, he could get Palmateer to fly him in. For some reason he couldn't imagine asking Bea. It would be summer before he would be able to afford a flight. And what good would that be?

Burl had been making a list of supplies: stovepipes, the tools he would need to break through the roof, and the stuff to patch up around the hole he made. He had some skills at carpentry, but the task seemed way too hard. The man at the hardware kept giving him more and more information until he thought his head would burst.

And there was no use heating a vaulted cabin unless he threw up some insulation between the rafters. That wasn't a hard job—the guy at the hardware had explained it to him—but it was another trip on the Budd car. Then there were food and supplies, ice-fishing equipment, a rifle.... Burl knew, growing up by the railroad, that you could take just about

<116>

anything in on the Budd car, but the path from Mile 29 to the cabin included steep hills. He would need a sled to drag stuff in once there was snow. He would also need muscles of iron—he wasn't sure where you bought those.

There were things he could collect from home. Things that were his. There was his canoe. Somehow, sometime, he would have to get that. But even if he was able to get his own stuff, he still needed cash. Bea's advance for clothing and food was the only money he had seen from her. He wasn't in a position to protest.

She never mentioned anything about Gow being his father. He wondered if maybe she had come to realize he was lying. Still, she looked at him in a funny, calculating kind of way.

She had cornered him and he had lied. But this lie, like no other, was a fierce wish. It happened in fairy tales all the time, the changeling child stolen from his real parents. And Nog had said they looked alike. If only. In the meantime, he concentrated his attentions on getting back to the camp.

He had asked Palmateer when he might get paid. Palmateer had shrugged. "She's got her own way of doing things, but don't worry, she won't cheat you. She had to scramble herself when she was a kid."

Burl worried anyway. If he had to go in a hurry, he'd sure like to have some money on him.

He dreamed about the Maestro. Burl was following him through a forest. "I've got *The Revelation*," he kept saying, but even though the Maestro looked back, he never slowed down.

Burl got up, unable to sleep. It was before midnight. He stared out at the bay, choppy under a relentless north wind. There would be snow on the wind's tail. That was the way Palmateer put it. The full moon cut herself free from the straggly clouds now and then. Burl could see the planes bobbing

< I I 7 >

at their moorage. Soon they would be hauled up, the pontoons replaced with skis.

Burl headed over to the couch. The *Reader's Digest Complete Do-It-Yourself Manual* lay open on the coffee table. It wasn't half complete enough, but it gave him something to dream about. There was a cup of instant decaf that he had been drinking earlier. It was stone-cold.

The door opened. It was Bea.

"Don't lay an egg!" she said.

"You scared me."

Bea sat down on the arm of the couch. "You look like a fox just entered the coop."

Burl managed a tight little smile.

"I'm glad you're up," she said, taking off her gloves. Burl closed his book and waited. He watched her eyes reading the title of the book on his lap.

"There was another show about the late Nate Gow on the radio." Bea undid the buttons of her coat. Then she rooted around in her purse and came out with a pack of cigarettes. She lit up. "Darn interesting," she said. "Reminiscences, bits of interviews—that kind of thing. It's funny listening to people talk about someone you've met. Guess it's the first time I've ever known anybody famous." She looked straight at Burl. It unnerved him a bit.

"I read all I could in the papers, *Maclean's* magazine. Watched a special on the TV, even. Nobody ever mentions any family. I mean, immediate family. No wife or kids." She paused. "Know what I mean?"

Burl glanced up. He had no fringe of summer-long hair to hide behind. Now would be the time to tell her. But he kept his silence.

"Don't you think it's about time we talked?" she asked.

"About what?"

< I I 8 >

"What you plan on doing now that he's gone?"

Burl looked into Bea's eyes for a clue as to what she was getting at. "I don't know what you mean," he said.

She leaned forward and stubbed out her cigarette in an ashtray on the coffee table. She leaned back, ran her fingers through her hair, shook her head a bit to get the dampness out, smoothed her hair back down.

"On the radio show tonight some old friend was talking about how much Gow enjoyed the north. He liked to drive up this way. Liked to get away from it all. Just hang out in a motel somewhere for a few days where no one knew him." She turned her gaze on Burl again. "Is that how it happened?"

Burl looked down at his book. He had been rereading the section on insulating a ceiling. He wished she would go and let him daydream about stapling up foam sheets, covering them with quarter-inch ply.

"You see pictures of him ten or twenty years back. Handsome guy. Energy just popping out of every pore." She glanced at Burl again. "I got to thinking. A young woman—a pretty young waitress, for instance—stuck in some dead-end whistlestop out on the highway—seeing nothing but truckers and salesmen all day. Then suddenly this guy steps out of a long black limo and heads in, starts to talk—could that man talk when he got his revs up! Takes a room in the motel for a few days . . ."

Maybe it was the smoke in the room, but Burl began feeling moths start whirling around in his head, his whole body. He wanted to go out into the wind, get a good hard whack of it in his nostrils.

Bea leaned a little closer.

"Who'd blame her, Burl? He'd be irresistible. Funny, sensitive, obviously well-heeled, even if he didn't dress the part. It

<119>

wouldn't be a crime. I mean, it's only human nature, what happened."

"What happened?"

"Jeez, Burl. For a sixteen-year-old, you're pretty wet behind the ears."

Bea picked up a cushion and poked him good-naturedly in the side of the head. Burl pushed the cushion away. He was beginning to put it together: Nathaniel Gow and some imaginary waitress falling in love.

"I don't know how it happened," he said.

"Oh, come on, Burl," she said. "I think you need to talk this out."

"There isn't anything to tell. I mean, no one ever really told me how it happened."

"But somehow," said Bea, careful now, seeing his distress, "somehow you got back together. Somebody contacted somebody. All I was trying to get at was that if you are his love child, that's not such a big deal these days. You don't have anything to be ashamed of. You know what I mean? *And*, if you are, you do have some rights, Burl. Or you *ought* to."

A love child. Burl had heard that expression before. Funny, how a child born to parents who were married was just a child. Out of wedlock, it was a love child. A love child reunited with his father.

"A person's got to stand up for his rights," she said. "You see why I'm concerned?"

Burl had not put this idea in her head. When he told Bea he was Gow's son, he was only confirming her suspicions. He couldn't tell her the real story. Anyway, he wanted to hold on to this dream for a bit longer. Like when you walk around in the department store holding on tight to something you can't afford, but it's yours to feel and smell and hold as long as you don't step out the door.

"I don't know what to do," he said.

"Well," said Bea in a self-satisfied way. "Maybe that's where I come in." She slid down from the arm of the chair onto the seat. She was all business now. Burl moved away from her a bit.

"I'm not sure anyone down there in Toronto knows about that cabin of yours—you see where I'm going with this, Burl? Gow let me know, more than once, that privacy was of the utmost importance to him. Believe me, I know when I'm being told to keep my big mouth shut. I got the feeling that maybe not even his nearest and dearest knew about it."

"He called it his folly," said Burl.

"Exactly," said Bea. "Maybe not his first, either." She raised her eyebrow again. Burl turned away, embarrassed.

"Anyway, there *it* is and here *you* are. And dammit—even if you don't get another red cent—that place should be yours, my friend."

She sounded indignant. She got up and walked over to the door to look out, almost as if maybe there was someone coming up the driveway right this minute with a deed in his hand.

"He built that place for you," she said. She sounded as if Gow himself had entrusted her with this fact. "What kind of arrangement did you two come to about the cabin?"

Burl put the book off his lap. "All he said when he left was not to chop up the piano for firewood."

"I bet he did," she said. "Nothing else? Nothing on paper?"

"Nothing. He was coming back."

"Right," she said. "I tried to figure what he was doing setting up that camp. I mean, he was about as at home in the wilderness as I would be on a concert stage. Then I met you and I began to put two and two together. When I heard that show tonight on the radio—the part about hiding out in the north now and then—the whole puzzle sorta came together. I'll bet dollars to doughnuts he meant Ghost Lake for you. It makes sense. He knew you wouldn't be happy down there in Hogtown. And maybe he didn't want anyone to know about you. I can understand that. So he builds this great camp where he can come and visit whenever he can get away."

Burl wanted her to go on and on. He had dreaded having to explain how he came to be the Maestro's son. Now Bea was doing it for him. All he had to do was nod. Then, suddenly, he realized the story was taking a nosedive.

"But now that he's gone, well, things might be murky on the legal end."

"Someone else might get it?" said Burl. The thought of anyone claiming the camp had never even crossed his mind. He went cold all over. It was his place now.

Bea looked him square in the face. "The thing is, once lawyers start digging around in his accounts in order to settle the estate, they're bound to come up with something. The deed to the land, for example; some hefty invoices—what does a piano like that cost? Twenty, thirty grand. Huh! I bought the Beaver for that much. Anyway, you can't spend that kind of cash and not leave a paper trail."

"But it was his money," said Burl. "He could do whatever he wanted with it."

"Sure. But he's gone and now other people have to decide what to do with what's left behind. It's not like pocket money, Burl. When an estate is being settled, folks want to know what's what and who gets it."

When Grandfather Robichaud died, Doloris got a gold fob watch on a chain. It had been willed to her; it came in the mail. She let Burl hold it sometimes. Then Cal took it and sold it, and Doloris hit him with a frying pan. That was in the days when she still had some pluck in her.

"I guess that's what will happen," said Burl.

"So?" said Bea. "What do you plan on doing about it?"

"I don't know."

"That's where Auntie Bea can help." She winked at him. Then her face got serious again. She picked her words with an uncharacteristic delicacy. "Can you get your mother in on this?"

Burl's apprehension showed on his face.

"Just asking," said Bea. "I guess she's not in the picture anymore."

"No," he said, allowing the story to grow but not daring to look at Bea while it did.

"Do you know if he supported her at all? If he did, there might be records."

"I don't think so."

"No support payments, eh? Didn't want the world to know about his little misadventure. Some backwoods chickie gets herself knocked up and claims the father is a big celebrity— who's gonna believe her?"

"It wasn't like that!" cried Burl.

"Okay, okay. Don't get your shorts in a knot." Bea leveled off her voice.

"She never told him about me," said Burl. "Not until she got sick. As soon as he heard he came."

"She got sick?"

Burl nodded. "She died. This summer."

"I see," said Bea. Then she was quiet for a moment. Respectful. "So there is no one, just like you said. His people should know that."

His people. The idea hadn't really registered on Burl. Gow might not have a wife and family, but he would have people. All he knew about was a friend named Reggie, and he seemed harmless enough. But people—the way Bea said it—they might try to steal the cabin from under his nose.

"Burl?" Bea was leaning close. "Listen to me." She seemed uncomfortable. "I see these crazy cases in the magazines sometimes. Rich relatives squabbling over who gets the cutlery. It's enough to make you sick. But if you are Nathaniel Gow's child—illegitimate or not—his family ought to know about it. You have a birthright."

Burl slumped back on the couch. He was exhausted.

"You look beat," she said. "We'll talk some more tomorrow."

"Okay," said Burl. Tomorrow sounded good.

She headed for the door, buttoning up her coat. She let in a great swirling eddy of snow-laced wind.

"You never know," she said, turning toward him. "Now that he's gone, the family might really be pleased to know there's something of him left behind. Something more than records, I mean."

< 1 2 4 >

The Plan

THE NEXT DAY THERE WAS work to do and Bea wasn't around much, not so you could take her aside and look her in the eye.

The shop needed a major cleanup, so Burl found himself on his own pushing a broom. He imagined his mother fifteen years younger working in a motel on the Trans-Canada. The fantasy failed when he tried to imagine her actually talking to the Maestro. Maybe they would just have taken a lot of Valium together.

Palmateer came by around five as the sun was setting. "She wants you up to the house," he said.

Bea was in a study off her living room. She was staring at her desk in a satisfied way. She picked up what was sitting there and brought it over to him for his inspection.

"Take a gander at this," she said.

<125>

It was a photograph of Gow when he was a teenager. It was in color, snipped from some magazine. His hair flopped over his forehead; his eyes were fiercely concentrating on something.

Burl knew he could look that way. He had seen his eyes staring back at himself in a mirror with that unwavering look. He studied the picture hard.

Then he handed it back to her. Maybe there was a bit of a smile on his face. A bit of longing that wanted to burrow right into those features. Bea seemed pleased with his reaction.

"Here's what I'm suggesting." Burl sat where she pointed, a low chair by the window. "I'll advance you the money to get down to Toronto." She said this as if Burl had driven a hard bargain but she had finally caved in.

"What?" he said. "Why?"

"Do you want Ghost Lake or not?"

"Yes . . . I mean . . . well, yes."

"Well, that's good," said Bea. "Because this is going to take some backbone, kid." She sat at her swivel chair, crossed her knees, and leaned back. "I'd fly you down if I weren't so busy. But, in a way, it's best you go yourself."

"But I wouldn't know what to do."

"I did a little digging," she said. "Gow usually paid for his shipments in cash. But the last charter, he used his credit card. You following me so far?"

Burl managed a halfhearted nod.

"So anyway, I phone up the credit-card folks and I spin them a little fib, say I've got a problem. I tell them I just finished making a big haul of supplies when I find out my client has died. So what am I supposed to do? They try to tell me it'll all be dealt with, and I tell them I'm sure it will but I ain't planning on waiting till Christmas to see if it's under my tree, you know what I mean?

<126>

"Well, the long and short of it is, they got me the address of Gow's attorney." Seeing no acknowledgment of a shared victory on Burl's face, Bea continued. "That means the *estate*: the folks you're going to have to introduce yourself to if you want what's yours."

Burl looked hard at Bea. He had wrestled with his conscience all day, but now he found his mind drifting to other matters. She was going to advance him the money for the trip. As if it were a present. He wasn't sure what a bus to Toronto cost, but the fact was, she owed him three weeks' pay minus the advances. She'd kept him on a string all along.

"Why are you doing this?"

Bea twiddled with a pencil on her desk. "I'm not going to bore you with my life story, kid, but I didn't have it easy. I know a little something about getting what you have coming to you." There was a sad look in the corners of her eyes. She blinked it away. "That's a kind of roundabout answer. Will it do for now?"

For a moment Burl felt something like affection for her. He nodded.

"Good," she said. She turned to her desk. There was a neat stack of papers there. "Toronto's a breeze. For a big city, it's easy to find your way around. Here's a map. I've already marked off where the bus depot is and the street where the lawyer's office is."

She got up and stood behind Burl, leaning over his shoulder and pointing each place out. "Walking distance," she added. "And here's the YMCA. It doesn't cost much to stay there. Mind you, this kind of thing isn't going to come together in any big hurry."

"I might have to stay there?"

She laughed. "A couple of days. If they'll see you. Then you can hightail it back here."

<127>

A couple of days. That didn't sound so bad. Ghost Lake was worth that. "And then it would be mine? I mean, if they believe I'm who I say I am?"

Bea whooped. "Burl, my boy. It doesn't work like that. Like I said, nobody's gonna hand this thing to you on a platter. You come back here. I'll support your claim. Then there'll be letters back and forth. Then they'll summon you back down there. More letters, more visits. Some kind of investigation. It could be years before they sort something like this out."

Burl felt the weight of it all crushing in on him.

"Here's your schedule out of Sudbury. There's a six-thirty bus that'll get you into Toronto by noon."

"I can't do it," said Burl. "I appreciate what you're trying to do for me, but there's no way."

Bea sighed. She took her seat again, leaned on one elbow, staring at him. Her gaze was relentless.

"You're frightened, right?"

He nodded readily.

"Well, that's good. You walk in there cocky, they'll throw you out on your ear."

"But I couldn't walk in there at all. I don't know anything about ... about him. About my mother and Nog, I mean."

"Nog?"

"It's what his friends called him," he said.

Bea seemed impressed. "You're wearing one of his shirts. You know a nickname I ain't run across in all my reading. That's the kind of thing that'll begin to convince them. You don't have to know much. But they will want to know *something* about how Gow and your mother got together. He didn't say anything?"

"Nothing."

"And your mom?"

Burl shook his head.

< 1 2 8 >

"Burl. You don't want to talk about this thing. Fine. In a crazy kind of way, the less you say the better. You're a missing kid no one is claiming. You're a nobody. The estate will try to prove you're somebody other than Gow's son. If they can't prove that, well, then they'll have to look at what's called the circumstantial evidence. You were living with him. He let you stay in the cabin, sent you supplies—that kind of thing. You see how it works?"

All Burl could think of was that he was a nobody right now. Unclaimed. He must have looked miserable, because Bea's voice softened.

"You think I'd expect you to do this all by yourself?" Her voice was amiable. "I'm gonna be here for you, kid. I've helped you so far, haven't I? I've got all the records of his phone calls, the invoices for the flights, the supplies he sent up to you. Comes close to a thousand bucks. That's a lot of dough to spend on a nobody."

He looked at her, and she held his gaze steadily. She could fly through anything. She was fearless.

"You have to put in an appearance first. That's all. You just say Gow said you should contact them if anything happened to him. I've got a feelin' they don't even know about Ghost Lake. Since you're not asking for anything else—not demanding a share of his millions—these folks may just hand you the place."

It wasn't what she had said before. But she called them folks, and that sounded a lot easier to handle than people. Burl tried to imagine talking to folks.

"I want to help you get up there," she said. "That's why I gave you the job here. I know you're just itching to get back. But first things first. You let them know you're around. Then back you come, and out to Ghost Lake. I'll fly you out. Palmateer's got an old stove that just needs the door welded

<129>

back on. We can get you set up just jim-dandy. The longer you're there, the more convincing your argument is. Possession is nine-tenths of the law. But we've got to start this business with the estate first. You know what I mean?"

She might as well have cast a spell over Burl. A woodstove. A flight back to Ghost Lake.

"Opportunity, kid," she said. "Maybe you're not used to what it looks like. So let me introduce you. Burl, this is Opportunity. Opportunity, this is Burl."

Burl smiled a little. Then a lot.

"That's what I want to see. What are you waiting for!"

<130>

The Nobody

BURL LAY IN HIS BED, heavy with indecision. He tried to figure out what he feared most: Bea and their shared lie, or the unknown forces in Toronto that controlled what was left of Gow in this world.

He rolled over. His sheet had balled up; his cheek lay against the worn and musty fabric of the couch. It had a waiting-room smell.

Cal and Doloris had not reported him missing. What was it now—just over two months. Cal wouldn't have told Doloris about the incident at the secret place, about Tanya. When Burl didn't return for dinner, his mother might have shouted from the door for him—"Burl. Burl?"—as if he were a dog wandered too far off on a good sniff. By the time she came

<131>

back to the table, Cal would have probably eaten his supper and Burl's, too.

Who else was there to know if he was gone? Who had noticed when his sister, Laura, died? He had been eight. Laura had been eleven. She had been run over, a drunk driver. He couldn't remember anyone at the funeral. Granny Robichaud wasn't even there.

Bea was right. He was a Nobody descended from a long line of Nobodies. It ran in the family. A Nobody couldn't go missing. It was impossible.

The Maestro had called him a wild child. Not a love child.

The couch bristled rough against Burl's face. He rolled over on his back, cupped his hands under his head. His scalp felt like it was crawling with fleas, but when he scratched, he realized that the vermin were inside his skull.

How hard would it be to play this game?

"You won't have to make things up," she'd said, as if she knew it was all a lie anyway.

"Listen," she'd said. "They don't believe you? You hang your head—you're good at that—and leave. Nothing lost, right? But—and this is important—if they ask about the cabin, you just throw it back in their face. 'What cabin?' you say to them. Give 'em some of their own medicine. You see? You've got something they want. But if they want it, they've got to consider the whole package."

She was too quick for him. First she had told him they would find out about Ghost Lake and take it from him. Now she was saying they would need him to find out about it.

What could he do? He could run away, but where? Besides, he wanted the money he had coming to him from Bea.

"There's something real sad about a person who dies leaving

<132>

no one behind," Bea had said. "People like the idea of immortality. That's you, Burl. You see what I'm saying?"

Immortality. That's what Gow had wanted. That's what the oratorio was all about. Something to leave behind.

"They don't buy it, we leave," Bea reiterated. "No calling in our lawyers to do battle—nothing scuzzy. No going to the press, although the estate might be afraid of that. We just see how willing they are to see Justice done, you know what I mean?"

Bea Clifford had obviously given the whole thing a lot of thought.

"It isn't as if you're asking for the world," she'd said. "Hell, tell them they can have the piano if they want it. Just so you can have Ghost Lake. Once they figure you're not a gold digger, maybe they'll let you have it. Get you to sign something saying you won't come back for more or go blabbing your story to the newspapers."

Millions? Was that what Bea wanted? And what was this about going to the newspapers? It was as if her plan were a huge house, and he'd only been shown the mudroom.

"Okay, okay. Stop aiming those headlights at me. You wanna know what's in this for Bea Clifford?" She'd relaxed a bit, smiled nicely. "Well, I'll tell you.

"You wanna live up there, right? Fine. But you know as well as I do that you'll still need money. That's where I come in. That lake's gotta be one of the most picture-postcard perfect spots I ever saw. Throw in a pyramid—well, it's a once-in-a-lifetime vacation paradise.

"So here's Auntie Bea's plan: if I can put a hunting or fishing party in that cabin of yours, maybe a family in the summer—that's a fine sandy beach you have there—for three weeks every season, a dozen or so weeks a year, you can make enough money to keep yourself in macaroni for the rest of

<133>

the time. People pay me to outfit them, fly them in. You get the rent. We both win."

He believed her. Oddly, he felt a little better knowing what she was really after. He didn't mind giving up the cabin now and then. As long as it was his. He would spend those times up in the miner's cabin.

And that's where it had ended. Except that it didn't end. Bea's words hatched and buzzed in his skull until he wished he could crack it open and let them out.

A truck rolled by on the Intervalle Road.

Weesbach. That was the bowhunter's name. Gord Weesbach. Burl wasn't sure his dad hung around with Gord much anymore, but he had a feeling Gord worked at the mill. Suddenly Burl could see it all too clearly: Gord tapping his father on the shoulder. "Seen that kid of yours lately, Cal?"

It wasn't as if Cal wanted him back. Burl didn't have any illusions about that. But you could never tell what Cal might do. He'd start thinking about how Burl had got one over on him—something like that—and it would drive him crazy. Soon enough he'd be around, causing trouble, wanting something.

Gord Weesbach was up north somewhere right now. Sitting in a tree waiting for bear. But only for the week. What choice did Burl have? He had to get out of Intervalle, but he didn't have any cash. Bea had seen to that. She'd been generous enough, but as far as she was concerned, Burl wasn't leaving Intervalle unless it was on a bus to Toronto.

He squeezed his eyes tight until they popped and fizzed with red fireworks. He could get up right now and leave. He could step out that door and be on the highway in half an hour. He wasn't a prisoner. He could hitch a ride to somewhere. Anywhere.

And that's when it came to him. A little bit of mercy. The

< 1 3 4 >

beginning of a plan all his own. He was too tired to give it any real consideration, but the thought of it released him from some of the knots he was tied up in. Allowed him to rescue a little consolation from what was left of the night.

Tomorrow was soon enough. Then the Nobody would work out the details of his own plan.

Koschei the Deathless

NATALIE AGNEW RAPPED on the warped and weathered door. It took her a minute to think where to knock, half-afraid of putting her fist clear through it. There were no signs of anyone at home. No half-starved hunting dog on a chain barking its head off—that's what she had expected to see when she first laid eyes on the Crow residence. There was no smoke coming out of the chimney pipe.

"Hello," she said. "Mrs. Crow?"

She stepped down from the stoop and walked through the frost-licked grass that grew knee-high around the shack. It had been trodden down in only one mean path from the oil-dead patch of red sand that must serve as a car park.

Natalie listened to hear if a car was coming. Nothing but the screech of blue jays. She peered through a window, squinting,

<136>

blocking the light out with her hands so that her eyes might sift the shadows inside for signs of life. Nothing.

She had phoned the high school in Vaillancourt, but Burl Crow had not registered for school there. She'd phoned the Catholic school in Ste. Chrodegang with the same result.

In the school records she'd found that Burl's parents had no phone service. So that was that, for a while. But then a Saturday came along and David had another appointment up at the reservation. So she had tagged along. Not for the weather this time. It was horrible, the ground cold and hard, the trees bleak. Winter in the wings.

Through the window she saw the remains of breakfast on the table: two bowls, a carton of milk, cornflakes, a thick brown mug, an empty Coke can. But from the look of the house, these things might have been sitting there for weeks.

She heard a car backfire up the road. She just barely made it back to the path before a huge old boat of a car squealed into the property, almost sideswiping her Tercel.

The man who climbed out from behind the wheel leered at her as he hitched up his belt under a formidable gut.

"Are you lost?" he said, leaning against the trunk of his car. His eyes were all over her. She folded her arms across her chest.

"I'm sorry," she said, and was instantly angry at herself for capitulating to this big lout of a man. She wasn't sorry at all. "I'm looking for Burl Crow."

The man jabbed his key into the trunk lock and turned it, never taking his eyes off her.

"He ain't here," he said. His thumb pushed the button to release the catch. The trunk opened with a screeching sound.

"Is this where he lives?" she asked.

The man reached into the trunk and pulled out a shotgun. Natalie gasped.

< 1 3 7 >

"He ain't here no more," he said. "Who are you anyway?"

Natalie took a few steps up the path toward him. There was no other way of getting to her car, and although she knew the gun was just for show, she wanted to be in the Tercel heading out the driveway in case he changed his mind. He cracked the gun open to see if it was loaded. He was toying with her. He had a rude smile on his face, now that he cradled a firearm. As she neared him he stepped forward so that she would have to go around him, detouring into the overgrown grass.

It annoyed her to think that this inflated, vulgar hulk might be Burl's father. "Burl was a gifted student of mine."

"Gifted!" the man snorted. "That's a good one."

"We'd lost touch."

He raised his eyebrows and leered again. "Foolish boy," he said. "You can bet I wouldn't lose touch."

Natalie stopped in front of him. He laid the gun across his shoulder and leaned a little out toward her, just in case she wanted to give him a kiss. He was very much closer to getting a slap across the face, but Natalie resisted the urge. He was dangerous. She could see that. And she could see, suddenly, a lot more. Things that had puzzled her about Burl suddenly had something like an explanation. Despite the man's menacing attitude, her rage grew.

"As a representative of the school board, I want to know where he is," she snapped.

He took a step back, covering his heart with his free hand.

"Well, so do I," he said. "Why don't you tell me where the boy can get in touch with you when he calls in?"

He pretended to cower again, raising his forearm across his face as though he expected a lashing for being so impertinent.

"Fine," she said, stepping past him and hurrying toward her own car. She found a piece of paper and wrote her name and

<138>

the school phone number on it. She handed it to him. With the open car door between them, she dared to speak again.

"In case Burl has run away, Mr. Crow, I'll make sure that the police have been alerted. I'm sure you took that step when he first left."

The little joke he had been having at her expense withered on his face. She saw his fist tighten around the stock of his gun.

"Why don't you mind your own friggin' business," he said.

"You can bet I will," she said, sliding into her seat, turning on the ignition, and revving the motor high. Then she rolled down the window and yelled, "Burl *is* my business." She didn't think there was much chance he heard her. She rolled the window up again fast.

He shouted something, too. She revved the motor higher so that the engine squealed. She put the car in gear. He leaned the gun against the rusted-out bumper of his car and, with his hands up, walked toward her.

She took her foot off the pedal and opened her window a crack. She'd already made sure the doors were locked.

He leaned down so that his lips were up against the crack where the window was open.

"He's gone to live with his grandma up in Dryden, since you're so concerned." His voice was even. "Things weren't working out here." He tried to sound a little sad, as if it had been a hard decision. Then he stood back. "There. Does that make us friends again?"

"We'll see," said Natalie, and her foot went down hard on the accelerator. The car flew into reverse; she turned the steering wheel wickedly. Then she screamed out of the garbage dump of a yard. She was out on the road, shivering and hugging the wheel close to her chest, before it crossed her mind that perhaps she had run over the horrible man's foot.

< I 3 9 >

A Night in the Shadow

THE BUS CRAWLED OUT of the terminal on Notre Dame in the dark of early morning. Despite the hour, Bea had driven Burl into Sudbury herself. She wanted to give him one last briefing.

He had stared out at the cratered moonscape that surrounded the city as they drove in from Intervalle. The fan in the Bronco was up high, blowing hot air in on the silence. There was no other sound. He saw the lights of the mines, an unexpected stream of traffic—a shift change. Pharaoh, where he had grown up, was only thirty miles away, but Sudbury might as well have been the moon for the number of times he'd traveled there. And yet, here he was traveling to Sudbury for the second time in as many days. Bea had brought him in the day before for some spook 'em clothes of his own. How convincing would it be for Gow's lost son to appear on the doorstep looking

< I 4 0 >

like a waif? There had been talk of another haircut, but his hair had grown long enough that it fell just like Gow's in the pictures of him as a child genius. So they left Burl's hair as it was, and he wore one of the Maestro's monogrammed shirts.

Bea bought him a round-trip ticket, good for any time. Then she grilled him once more. He was to phone as soon as he had seen the lawyers. She explained to him about long-distance phone calls. She didn't miss a thing. Finally, when he was at the door, she handed him an envelope. She held it out of his grasp for one last moment.

"I could have arranged with my bank for you to pick this up at a branch in Toronto, but I trust you, Burl." He could see in her eyes just how far she trusted him: about as far as a man can hurl a moose, as his father liked to say.

When he was on the bus, he counted the money. She had said there would be enough for expenses and a room at the Y for a week. But the cash didn't add up to what he had earned working at Skookum.

Somewhere past Noble, the moon still in the sky, Burl realized that he was glad Bea had shortchanged him. He didn't want to feel he owed her anything. It was kind of like freedom.

He drifted off to sleep.

He sat up several hours later, groggy and disoriented, to find himself barreling down Highway 400 into Toronto. There seemed to be a thousand lanes of speeding traffic stretching out to either side.

Then they were at the Bay Street Terminal, and he was disgorged from the bus like a frog from the belly of a hooked bass. He stood with his spook 'em clothes all wrinkled at the knee in the middle of what appeared to be Chinatown and stared at his map. He had stashed his duffel bag in a locker at the bus station. It cost him a buck, but he wasn't planning

< 1 4 1 >

on heading to the Y just yet. Nor was he planning on seeing
any lawyers.

He was looking for Spadina Road.

Toronto was nothing like the postcards. Or maybe it was the
parts of it you couldn't show in a picture that got to Burl:
the high-pitched bleep of a truck backing down an alley, the
air brakes of a bus, people squabbling in foreign languages, a
panhandler sobbing in no fixed language at all. The urgent
wail of an ambulance threading its way through the river of
traffic.

Gow had called the city the Shadow. And that was how
Burl saw it, in all its darkness and unfamiliarity.

A girl with a shaven head and nose rings played the violin
on a street corner. Burl stopped to watch her. She was beautiful
in her short black dress and her legs pale as birch bark. She
played feverishly. She saw nothing, her eyes rolled into her
head as if reading some music there. Then she stopped, and
she looked like someone who had just woken up. In a daze,
she stooped and counted the change people had thrown into
her case. She stowed her instrument and headed up the street,
her clogs clapping. She carried the case under her arm, and a
cigarette flapped from her black-penciled lips. She looked back
furtively a couple of times.

She yelled at Burl, told him to stop following her. He let
her pull ahead.

Smells pressed in on him. Exhaust and cooking fat and dusty
dry goods for sale, piled in toppling heaps on the sidewalk, and
fresh tar and last night's vomit frozen, now melting.

Burl saw in an hour more people than he had seen in his
whole life. His eyes smarted with the strain of seeing and the
stinging stench of the yellow air. His head ached with the

< 1 4 2 >

blare and discord. His feet ached with the unrelenting hardness of concrete.

He bought a sausage on a bun from a street vendor. He sat on the sill of a bank window until the pigeons got too pushy. He had never seen a pigeon before. He had never seen a bird with so little self-respect.

In the doorway of an out-of-business store with its windows newspapered over, a woman slept in a blanket.

Spadina Avenue was only a few blocks from the bus terminal. But that wasn't Spadina Road, and there was a lot of the avenue before he got to the road and then a lot of the road before he reached his destination. The road climbed upward from the hullabaloo of outdoor markets. There were apartments and then houses and trees, fenced in like huge tired animals to protect them from lumbering out into the traffic. Burl walked until there was hardly anyone on the street. Then, near the peak of the hill, Spadina made a graceful curve, and there sat a castle. Casa Loma. Exactly like a postcard. There was something reassuring in that.

It was three o'clock before Burl finally crossed St. Clair and saw that the numbers were getting closer to the building he was looking for. He found it at last in a part of town called Forest Hill Village.

There were people here, shopping with baskets on their arms. In a single block there were four bakeries featuring elaborately braided loaves and cakes topped with glazed fruit. There was a market store in which the apples appeared to have been individually polished. There was a restaurant called a *ristorante*. The waiters in the *ristorante* were all thin with black hair.

Finally he reached the Columbine. That was the name on the return address of Reggie Corngold's letter.

The Columbine sat across the street from a little park. The

<143>

apartment house was four floors high, brown brick, ivy-covered. The doorway was impressive, with the name carved above solid wooden doors painted black like the entrance to a church. There were six windows set in each door. There was a sign warning tradesmen to use the rear entrance.

Burl stepped into the hallway, not knowing what to do. There were eight tiny mailboxes there. He checked the names. Corngold was number five. There was no mail in the box.

Burl was just about to start up the stairs when he heard footsteps descending. He backed up and waited. A woman, her high heels clicking resoundingly, passed by him and pushed at the heavy door with her briefcase. Burl helped. She smiled in a frowny kind of way, as if she was annoyed at herself for not paying enough attention to what she was doing. "Thanks," she said without looking at him, then clicked down the stairs to the street.

Feeling a little more reassured, Burl mounted the staircase in search of number five. No one home. But it was almost four o'clock by then. People would be off work soon. He decided to wait outside in the park, where he could see the residents arriving home. As he descended the staircase, the front door opened and his heart leaped, but it was only a postman. Watching from the stairs, he saw the postman open the whole panel of mailboxes with a key. There was an envelope for Reggie Corngold that he could not jam into the box, so he left it on the ledge below.

When the postman had gone, Burl held the envelope in his hand, wanting to open it, wanting to know something—anything—about this man who was Nog's friend. Then he placed it back on the ledge and pushed through the door.

Night was already falling. In the park there was a sign showing a little dog with a pile of poop behind it on the ground. The picture showed a shovel and a wastebasket. Burl

< 1 4 4 >

looked around. The sign worked. There was no dog poop anywhere.

He sat on a bench. A gust of wind blew a placard against his leg. It was another sign: PESTICIDES IN USE. PLEASE KEEP OFF. He didn't know where this new sign had come from. What was he supposed to keep off? He decided it didn't really matter. There were too many signs in the city as far as he could tell. If you paid attention to all of them, you'd go crazy.

After another cold hour, only one person had entered the Columbine, a fancy-looking lady in furs with a small dog under her arm. Then an elderly man arrived from around the side of the building, stuffing his car keys in his pocket. He had nice silver hair. Burl thought he would make a good friend for the Maestro. Burl skittered across the street to watch him claim his mail. Mr. Coffee, number three.

Soon all but number one and number five were safely home for the evening. Burl caught glimpses of the other tenants in their windows: T. Pollack was having a glass of beer. S. Braithwaite was watching television and eating something from a bowl. And F. Lonsdale seemed to be lighting a fire. All the Columbine dwellers were settling in for the night, while the night itself settled in, cold and damp.

At seven-thirty, Burl wandered back down to Forest Hill Village and found somewhere that wasn't a *ristorante* where he could sit and have a coffee and something to eat. He killed almost an hour, then ventured up the road to the Columbine, his heart pounding. There was still nobody in number five.

He stepped outside again. The wind had picked up. He dug his hands deep into his pockets. The woman in the furs was walking her little white dog in the park. The dog had a dump, and the woman, with a great effort, bent down to scoop it up. She used a plastic bag. When she crossed the street, dragging the dog with her, she glared at Burl.

< 1 4 5 >

There was no way he could sit in the park now—it was too cold—so Burl set off south to St. Clair. He walked west along St. Clair until he found a fast-food joint. He went in. There were black people there. He'd never seen one in the flesh.

Ten o'clock was the very latest he dared try number five. But when he got back to the Columbine, he could see that the lights were not on and the envelope was still sitting on the ledge in the hall.

There was, by then, no place open in the village, so Burl set off to see the city. He had slept several hours on the bus that morning, but he was quite tired. Still, he had no intention of spending any of his money staying at the Y. He thought of Bea waiting by the phone back in Intervalle.

There were lots of places open. He had heard that about cities, but it shocked him. And as he journeyed on into the night, he found that he liked it better than the day. So many other people looked as if they were out of place. He didn't stand out so much. He wondered if these night people had all just arrived in Toronto that day and had no place to stay.

It snowed a bit around four-thirty A.M. The snow seemed to warm things up a bit. He caught a night bus to St. Clair West, and—twenty-four hours after boarding the bus in Sudbury—he arrived again at the Columbine. Nobody's lights were on. He didn't go in. He found a retaining wall in the alley entrance to the parking lot, where he could see the windows of Reggie Corngold's apartment. A raccoon came by, looking for garbage. It didn't seem to mind Burl being there. With fascination Burl watched the hooded burglar tip the top of a garbage can and mess around inside, then sit there munching, its eye on Burl, while Burl sat shivering. It was fatter than any coon he'd seen in the bush. Probably lived on junk food.

They were still sitting there like that, although Burl was

< I 4 6 >

slumping by then, when the first hint of morning snuck down the narrow alley. Numbly Burl watched the dark begin to seep out of things, leaving them gray and lifeless, sucked dry.

Suddenly the raccoon startled and waddled off through a gap in the fence. It took Burl's dim brain longer to hear the car. He curled up small in the bushes. The car passed down the alley and turned into the parking lot behind the Columbine. Burl watched through the snarl of shrubbery. It was the woman he had seen leaving the building when he had first arrived. He had opened the door for her. She passed by, not seeing him in the shadows. He followed her. When the front door closed behind her, he ventured up to watch her through the windows. She stood in the front hallway and took off her black gloves. She opened mailbox number five. Burl was paralyzed. The woman picked up the envelope off the ledge and started tearing it open as she headed for the stairs.

Burl's first thought was that she was stealing Reggie's mail. Then it occurred to him that maybe she was Reggie's wife. And then, like a jolt of electricity passing through him, he knew without knowing why that *she* was Reggie. Reggie was a she. The letter, which he knew almost by heart now, shifted in his brain, as if each word were suddenly a different color than before, and made a different kind of sense.

By the time he recovered from this surprising turn of events, Reggie Corngold was halfway up the stairs. Unable to wait another moment, Burl swung open the heavy black door. She had already reached the first landing, her briefcase tucked under her arm, reading whatever had been in the oversize envelope. Startled by the sudden noise, she swung around.

"It's all right!" said Burl. His voice sounded too loud, husky from a night without talking.

Gathering her briefcase to her chest, she stepped down a single step. It squeaked noisily in the sleeping building.

< I 4 7 >

Burl cleared his throat. "I'm looking for Reggie Corngold," he said. His voice echoed.

She spoke cautiously. "What do you want?"

Burl leaned against the door, his hand on his chest, his mouth gaping open like a man who had run a marathon.

"I'm ... I'm a friend of Nog's."

"Who?"

"Nathaniel Gow."

She stepped down another step. Her eyes were wide. "You called him Nog." She was staring at him in an almost frightened way. Her face was thin; her eyes seemed far too large in such a slim face. Burl wished that he could say something to ease her mind.

"I don't know you," she said.

"I need to talk to you about him."

She stepped another step closer. "Nathaniel Gow is dead," she said. "I'm not going to stand talking to a complete stranger about him or anything else at this hour of the morning." Then, with a firm grasp of the banister, she turned and began again to climb the stairs.

"Please don't go," said Burl.

"Shhh!"

"I'm sorry," he whispered. "I've been waiting for you all night."

It was not the right thing to say. Without taking her eyes off him, Reggie backed up the stairs until her face was lost in shadows.

"I can explain," said Burl.

"Then phone me," she whispered, leaning over the banister. "I'm listed."

Burl moved to the foot of the stairs just as she rounded the corner above. "When?" he demanded.

She sighed. "Noon." She sounded exasperated.

< 1 4 8 >

The stuffy heat of the little lobby sapped the last bit of strength from Burl as Reggie tiptoed out of sight. Burl waited. After a long five minutes, he gave up, opened the front door, and stepped out into the cold.

He made his way around back to the service entrance. There was a stairway there to the basement. As quietly as he could, he went down, not daring to turn on the light. He bumped into walls wherever he turned. It was like a maze, but even if there had been a monster at the heart of it, he would not have turned back. He tripped over some boxes and landed on something soft—old clothes. Sleep, like a heavy door, closed down on top of him.

< 1 4 9 >

Reggie Corngold

A HEAVY DOOR NUDGED OPEN. Someone was playing the piano. The Maestro.

"What are you doing here?" Burl asked with a snarl. The Maestro only mumbled. Burl reslung his hammer in his work belt. "I can't strap in this insulation while you're playing," he said. But Gow didn't stop, just hunkered down into a difficult passage, as if he were a race-car driver heading into a series of hairpin turns. "You're just plain inconsiderate," Burl said. "After all, I'm the one going to all the work winterizing this place. Take that thing outside, before I swat you." Gow laughed. The threat only made him run further into the music, like a toddler escaping its mother by running deeper into the playground.

So Burl had to push him out, piano and all. Then he went back in and started to work again. He felt bad, though. The

<150>

snow was thick on the deck. He mustn't leave him there for very long. Must get the insulation done soon. Then he thought, Reggie will look after the Maestro. And sure enough, when he looked out the window, she was with him and had wrapped a large blanket around his shoulders. There was a cap of snow on his head. Reggie's hair was pale blond now. Which is the color her hair should be, thought Burl. With a name like Corngold.

A car honked. Tires squealed. A bus pulled noisily from a stop. Burl woke up. He had made himself a comfortable nest, although his bedding smelled of dust and mildew. He was at the end of a short corridor with chest-high walls. By the light filtering in from a small window at street level, he could see that the basement was divided into storage spaces. One per tenant.

He had no watch. He wondered if it was anywhere near noon. He wondered if it was even the same day. He sat listening to the creaking building above him, footsteps, the sound of traffic drifting down to him, and the unmistakable sound of a piano.

He sat up, stiff from a night of walking. Then he climbed up the back stairs and slipped out into a brisk but sunny day. The sun seemed quite high. He asked a man on the street the time. It was after noon. He didn't phone. He went directly to number five. He knocked three times.

"What do you want?" she said through the door. Burl slid her letter to Nog under the door and waited.

She gave him orange juice, freshly squeezed. She had the radio on to a classical station where people wrote in with requests. She made coffee. She made muffins as well. She didn't follow

< 1 5 1 >

a recipe. She added a bit of this and a bit of that and stirred. She cut up apples with long nimble fingers.

She moved around the kitchen in her bare feet. She was in old jeans, threadbare at the knee, and an extra-large starched blue-and-white-striped shirt. Her hair was wet from a shower, combed back straight. Last night she had been all in black: her coat, high-heeled boots, stockings, earrings, what he could see of a turtleneck sweater—all black, her hair the blackest thing of all.

She was pretty, Burl thought. Younger than Gow. He had never seen a woman so exotic. Last night she had seemed older. She had worn dark makeup, a little sorry looking, worn out. Now her face was clean and her eyes were as shiny as a painted turtle's shell. The sunlight coming through her window picked up a reddish tinge in her hair. She had been playing the piano when he knocked at her door.

"Where did you get this?" she asked as she let him in.

"At his camp. His place up north."

"Camp?"

"Ghost Lake."

She looked at him, amazed. "Noggy camping?" She smirked. "You've got to be kidding."

So he told her about the cabin. That was easy. She carved up apples, listening intently.

She laughed out loud at the thought of Noggy strolling through the bush to the train with his suitcase.

Her laughter and the warmth of her kitchen unwound Burl a bit. He explained about coming down on the bus the day before. He told her about the violinist on Spadina, and how he had never seen so many people walking around in the night, and it made him think of how Nog had called it the Shadow. Then he realized he was talking too much, and he clammed up.

<152>

"Ghost Lake," she said thoughtfully.

Then she told him why she had been getting home at six in the morning. She was a producer for CBC Radio. She was packaging a show. The night was the best time for that kind of work—no one around. Alone with her tapes. Except when Noggy used to come around. He sometimes worked on his own radio projects at the station. He was a night bird, too. That's how they had met.

She poured the muffin batter into the tins and placed them in the oven.

"When did you last see him?" she said.

He told her.

"How was he?" she asked.

Burl shrugged. "Up and down."

It was as if he had said something very clever. "Oh," she said. "I know—believe me, I know."

So they talked about Baron von Liederhosen conducting an orchestra from the deck, and they talked about the drugs. He didn't tell her what he had done with the drugs.

He told her about the bear. Her eyes grew huge with alarm and then a kind of wild delight and then concern. "It was lucky you were there," she said. And then, quickly, "Why were you there?"

"I had been . . . looking for him," said Burl.

"Why?"

"My mom was sick. She told me about him. She told me . . . to go to him."

In this way Burl ventured cautiously into the territory of his story. It was like a creek with a loon-shit bottom giving way under each step.

Reggie washed the cooking things in the sink. The muffins in the oven filled the air with cinnamon.

"I did a double take when I saw you," she said. The room

<153>

grew quiet. Burl played with the salt and pepper shakers. He noticed there was no clink of dishes in the water. He turned to look at Reggie. Her arms were still in the water, locked straight, the muscles standing out. Her back was to Burl, her shoulders clenched tight. He wondered if she was crying.

"Do you think I look like him?" he asked, very quietly, like the Maestro murmuring under his breath while he played. She heard him. She looked at him, and he tried to be the Maestro for her. She showed no sign of recognition. No sign of any emotion he could understand.

He saw her jaw tighten just for a moment. He could see the pulse in her long neck. Her eyes were shining. There might even have been a bit of a smile behind the curtain of her face, waiting to come out and dance a little number on her lips.

The timer on the stove buzzed.

"Done." She wiped at her cheek with the back of a soapy hand. Maybe there had been a tear. She dried her hands. She found oven mitts and took the muffins out of the stove. She made up a tray with the coffee things and muffins on a sunshine-yellow plate. There were two yellow napkins. "Come on," she said. She led the way into her living room.

Burl had never been in such a beautiful room. The furniture was new looking, the floor polished oak. The sun shone through salmon-pink draperies, making the oak glow like the embers of a fire. There were framed paintings and prints and photographs on peach-colored walls. There was a wall of bookshelves and rows and rows of records and compact discs and tapes. There was a white piano—not a grand like Gow's, but a low upright with a vase of blue flowers on it. There was a rug of many blues, like waves on a pebbly shore. Upon it stood a glass table, and on the table sat the briefcase he had seen her carrying, now open, with papers spilling out of it.

There was a tall black walking-stick-like creature frozen and

< I 5 4 >

camouflaged to look like a floor lamp shining down from behind a sand-colored chair. Reggie sat there.

Across the table there was a fat couch like a sandstone boulder softened by a million years of rain. There were plump cushions on it encased in material the color of a hummingbird's neck. Burl sat there gingerly. She placed the tray on the table between them, pushing her work aside with her naked foot. She poured coffee. Into it she poured hot, frothy milk. When she handed him the cup, her gaze drifted from his eyes to the monogram on his shirt.

Burl traced the initials with his finger. He suddenly felt uncomfortable in the shirt, though it was the softest thing he had ever worn. The muffins were too hot. Burl ate one all the same.

"Please," she said in her gentlest voice. "Now will you tell me why you are here."

Burl's mouth was full. He swallowed. "I came because of the letter."

"I know that. But why?"

"Because I'm supposed to go see his lawyers. But I wanted to talk to somebody who was a friend of his first. I haven't met any of his people. I'm kind of afraid."

This was easy to say. Everything was the truth. He felt as if he had just landed on a safe square in a hazardous board game. There was another pause. Without looking up, he could feel her staring at him. He didn't want to lie anymore, not to her. He wanted her to decide he was Nog's son by herself so that he could go on pretending.

"When people see lawyers, it's usually because they want something."

Burl took another muffin. Said nothing. Then he looked up. "I want the camp," he said. "That's all I want. I think he would want me to have it." His voice cracked when he said

<155>

it. He looked away hopelessly. How could he have dreamed even for a minute he could pull this off.

He heard the clink of her cup returning to her saucer. She was watching him.

"He was going to . . . bring me down here," said Burl. "He was coming up again in October to fetch me. He'd already chartered a plane—"

"Hah!" she interrupted him. "Nog flying?"

"No. For supplies," cried Burl. Her voice had gone hard, and he didn't want it to. "He takes the train in. I said that already. He's afraid of flying. I know that."

"Go on." Her voice still sounded as if she was testing him.

"I was staying up at the cabin. I didn't even know he had died until the floatplane came back up. That's Bea Clifford. She runs the airline. You can talk to her if you don't believe me."

"And this Bea person—she's the one who wants you to talk to the lawyers?"

Her voice was gentle again, but penetrating.

"Look," said Burl nervously. "I don't want to be here. In the city, I mean. I just want to be up there. I don't want to bother anyone. But I don't want anyone to take it away. I've never had anything until now. He wanted me to have it. It was like he built it for me. A place where we could get to know each other. Then he would have brought me down here to meet his folks. He was just . . . just . . ."

"Just getting up the courage?"

Burl looked at her to see if this was a trap. Then he allowed himself to nod a bit.

Reggie looked at him shrewdly. He blushed.

She looked away again, shaking her head. She was way off in her own thoughts. Then she laughed a little. "Nog roughing it," she said.

<156>

This sounded to Burl like safer ground. "He wasn't really. There's even a grand piano."

She seemed very surprised. Obviously she knew nothing about it. Some more of her doubt seemed to be peeled back a little bit. He began to think that she wanted to believe him.

"This morning," she said, "when I saw you in the lobby, I had the strangest feeling you were him. He was likely to turn up at the most outrageous times."

Burl had eaten two muffins already. Now he reached for another. Her glance shifted to his hand, and she took it in hers. Her hands were soft and creamy smooth. He didn't know what to do. She fingered the cuff of his right sleeve. "This button," she said.

"What?" he asked, fearful that he had given himself away somehow.

"I sewed this button on. Look." She brought both his wrists together and compared the buttons. The original was like pearl. The one Reggie had sewed on was much more yellow. "It was the best I could do."

A horn honked loudly outside. She released him. He didn't take the muffin. He leaned back, his hands clasped on his lap.

"What am I supposed to do with you?" she asked.

Burl shrugged. All he had wanted to do was to try out his disguise on someone named Reggie who had been a real friend of the Maestro's. Who knew what would happen next? "It's Ghost Lake," he said. "It's all I want in the whole world."

Reggie regarded him tenderly. "I'm not sure what to say, Burl. This is all so strange. You seem to be saying that you are his son. Is that what you're saying?"

Burl swallowed hard. He jerked his head up and down.

Reggie regarded him. "His illegitimate son."

Again Burl nodded. It was all out now. There was no going back.

<157>

He couldn't tell if she believed him or not. She sipped at her coffee. "He did come out of his coma once or twice before he died. A couple of relatives, close friends spoke to him. Colin saw him quite a bit. That's his lawyer. He was also an old friend. I was away in Vancouver. I never got to see him at the end. But he certainly never mentioned anything about a son to me."

She checked to see if Burl had registered this information. "So your friend Bea is right. Colin is your best bet."

Burl hated the sound of these people who had talked to Gow when he was dying. His real friends. People he had known all his life. How could Burl expect anything when he had only known the Maestro one day? One day.

Then he thought of the trip Gow was planning to make back to the camp. Desperately he clung to this thin strand of hope. Maybe he was coming for Burl. Maybe he had said something about him. Maybe he did want Burl to have the cabin.

He shuddered.

"Are you cold?" asked Reggie.

"No," he said. "Scared."

He had imagined being tricked, found out, cornered. He had imagined having to run. It had never occurred to him that being accepted, even a little bit, would be so hard to take. Keep thinking of Ghost Lake, he told himself. The lake, the lake, the lake. If he could just have the lake.

Reggie was watching him. A telephone rang. She answered it. The phone was cordless. Burl had never seen such a thing.

It was someone called Bernie who wanted to know how she was doing on a script. The script wasn't with the work on the glass table. "It's in my office," she said to the man on the phone. She started heading out of the room.

"Help yourself," she said to Burl. "I'll only be a minute."

He heard her walk down the apartment hallway. A door opened and closed. Burl looked around. His gaze landed on the piano. It was the first piano he had seen since he left Ghost Lake. He stretched out his fingers. Did they still remember the opening passage to the "Silence in Heaven"? He peeked down the corridor first. He couldn't even hear Reggie's voice anymore. He got to his feet and made his way to the sleek ivory-colored instrument.

Could he play the same tune on a white piano? He sat and placed his fingers where the Maestro had shown him. He pressed his foot down on the sustain pedal and then his fingers on the keys as quietly as possible. He remembered the chords perfectly. He played them again in a stately progression. He heard the door open down the hall, but he did not stop. He didn't want to talk anymore. He wanted Reggie to hear him play.

<159>

The Score

HE WAS AWARE OF REGGIE leaning on the edge of the piano. He had played his few chords through half a dozen times. It was his best performance ever.

"I'd like to hear more," she said.

"I don't know any more. That's all he taught me."

"Who taught you?"

"The Maestro."

Reggie looked inquisitively at him. "Do you mean Nog? Nathaniel Gow? He never took on students."

Burl shrugged. "He said if he taught me something, I'd have to call him Maestro. And that's what I call him."

"Gifted pianists from all over the world have begged him to become their master," said Reggie. "He turned them all away. Shooed them home to Oslo and Rio and Vladivostok."

Burl felt strangely elated. He placed his fingers on the keys again, but now he was far too shy to play.

"What is it he's taught you, then?" said Reggie. "I don't recognize it."

"It's the 'Silence in Heaven,'" said Burl. "From *The Revelation*."

Reggie wandered across the room to replace the telephone. "Who's it by?"

Burl turned on the piano stool. "By him," he said with some surprise.

Reggie stared at him. "What did you say?"

"The Maestro. It's part of his oratorio."

Reggie came to him. She was grinning; her eyes were glowing. She laid a hand on his shoulder. "Run that by me again, very slowly."

So Burl repeated what he had said. "It's from the Bible. The Book of Revelation."

She closed her eyes. Her fingers unconsciously massaged his bony shoulder. She took a deep breath. "Please let this be true."

"It *is*," said Burl.

Her hand tightened on his shoulder. Then she pulled it away.

"He used to talk about doing something big," she said. "I think he once talked about the Book of Revelation. But there was never any time."

"That's because of the Shadow," said Burl.

"The Shadow," she said. She let out a merry whoop of laughter. It seemed to surprise her; she covered her mouth. Then she walked away from him, slapping her hands against her legs. He watched, mesmerized. She stood at the window overlooking Spadina Road. She swung around.

"You have no idea, do you, how important this could be?"

Burl scratched his head.

< 1 6 1 >

"How much of it is there?" she demanded.

He remembered the old briefcase stuffed every which way, but a lot of the stuff in the case had been notes or sketches or rejected bits. He had looked through what he had thought was the good copy of the score. "More than a hundred pages," he said. It came back to him. "All of the parts are there, I think. But some of the movements are only sketched in." That was what the Maestro had said.

"Oy!" said Reggie.

It was dawning on Burl that *The Revelation* changed everything somehow. Now he had something to give.

"Burl," she said. "Listen to me."

She walked over to her record shelves. She indicated one shelf. "This is all Nathaniel Gow. I have something like fifty of his recordings. There are over ninety, not to mention reissues in compact disc. Do you know how many of these recordings are of his own work?"

"Music he wrote?"

"Yes. How many?"

Burl shook his head. "I don't know." Reggie had been fingering through the collection. She drew out one album. She held it up between her hands. "This," she said.

Burl walked over to look at the album she was holding. There were two records in it, featuring four pieces. "Nathaniel Gow: The Northern Suite." "The First Quartet." "The Piano Sonata in F sharp Major." And "Street Music: Twelve Variations on a Theme by Orlando Gibbons."

"Orlando," said Burl. "Like in his name?"

"What?" said Reggie. "Oh, yes. His mother decided before he was born that he was going to be a musician, and she named him after the great British composer Orlando Gibbons. Gibbons was one of Noggy's favorite composers.

"But, Burl, the point is that our Noggy was one of the truly great musicians of this century, a great pianist, a world-class conductor, an important interpreter of other people's stuff. But you are holding in your hands *all of the original compositions of Nathaniel Orlando Gow.*"

Burl wasn't sure what to think. He read the album cover again. Four pieces. That was all. There were times marked beside each composition. The longest was twenty-three minutes. The way the Maestro had spoken of *The Revelation*, it always sounded to him as if it would last a lifetime.

Reggie took the album from him and placed it back on the shelf. She led him to the couch. She sat beside him, holding both his hands in hers as if he might escape.

"Tell me about it, Burl. Please. It's an oratorio?"

"Yes." Then Burl remembered something the Maestro had said about it being his *Messiah*.

"So it is big," she said. "For chorus and soloists and a full orchestra."

"He said when it got performed, there wouldn't be a fiddle player out of work in all of Canada."

Reggie was delighted. "And you say it's mostly complete?"

Burl nodded. Caught up in her enthusiasm, he found himself recalling bits and pieces of what the Maestro had said. About the beginning being called "Patmospheres," and it sounding like an island under a blazing sun with buzzing insects, even a goat.

Reggie hung on every word, sometimes squeezing his hands in hers. He found himself searching for more and more things to say so that she would not let go of him.

She would interrupt with some remembrance of Nog, so that Burl felt they were talking about a mutual friend about whom he had some news. Finally, when he had racked his brains and there was nothing left to remember, she leaned back to examine his face. "You could almost be his son," she

<163>

said. "Almost. I can see this scared little boy looking out at me from your eyes. I used to see that in his eyes sometimes."

"I want to learn how to play the whole *Revelation*," said Burl. "Maybe if I brought it here, you could teach me." He looked hopefully at her.

Her eyes lit up, then suddenly she turned away, leaned forward, and picked up crumbs from the glass table. "I don't want you to be angry with me," she said. "But while I was in my office, I phoned Noggy's lawyer."

She glanced over at Burl. He sat very still.

"Colin knew Gow had been going up north a lot over the last year or so, but he knew nothing about the cabin. He was very interested. When I told him about you, he was even more interested. But he suggested I inform you about DNA testing. Do you know what that is?"

Burl was staring straight ahead. He wasn't sure what DNA testing might be, but he could guess. The fairy tale was well and truly over.

"Apparently scientists can tell just from a sample of blood— from a fingernail, even—whether you share Gow's genetic makeup. Amazing, isn't it?"

Burl nodded, but he didn't look at her.

"You think you'd want to go through that kind of thing?"

Burl shook his head violently.

"It's okay," she said soothingly. She patted him on the leg. "Burl, look at me, please."

He did. She didn't look angry. "Burl. I can't speak for the estate. But if you can lay your hands on *The Revelation*, a lot of people are going to be very, very pleased with you. And they're going to have to find some wonderful way of thanking you."

The Quest

REGGIE TOOK BURL to the bus station. She wanted to come with him, but business commitments made the trip impossible until the following week, and she was determined that the score be rescued as soon as possible.

"Mice!" she said. She remembered going to her family's cottage as a kid and finding that mice had made nests of Kleenex and newspaper and any other paper they could sink their teeth into. Her eyes filled with horror at the thought of *The Revelation* becoming a bed, a birth clinic!

She became almost panicky. Couldn't his friend Bea Clifford fly him in? Reggie would put up the money herself. Burl was reluctant to get back in touch with Bea, but he couldn't explain this to himself, let alone to Reggie. So, with her breathing down his neck, he phoned Skookum and got Palmateer. He was just about to take a party up to Kapuskasing, a long trip,

<165>

and he was planning on staying overnight due to a storm warning in the area. Bea had driven off in her spook 'em clothes to Nipissing University in North Bay to give a talk of some kind. He wasn't sure when she'd be back, but not until late. Burl wasn't sure if Palmateer knew anything about where he was or what he was up to. He left no message for Bea.

But there was a bus leaving Toronto at five o'clock that day, arriving in Sudbury at about eleven. He already had a ticket. So, reluctantly, Reggie settled for that. He told her about the Budd car, how he could get up there in the next day or two. Bea would pick him up at the bus terminal, he told her. He gave her the phone number for Skookum Airways.

Finally he was on board, and Reggie was waving to him as the bus pulled out. He liked her, all right, but he was glad she couldn't come. He needed to do this thing alone. Anyway, the cabin at Ghost Lake had never been meant for sharing. The Maestro had built it to get away from everyone, even his friends.

Burl leaned his head against the cold glass and watched the five o'clock tide of traffic carry the bus as slowly as a water-logged tree through the inner-city dusk. The Shadow. This was what Gow had been escaping. How hard it must have been for him to have Burl crash in on his solitude. Burl had driven him off. Perhaps now he could make some small amends for that.

It was snowing in Sudbury when he arrived. A freak storm had swept down from James Bay, blanketing the north in snow.

Burl took some of the money Bea had given him for the Y and found a cheap hotel near the bus depot. The proprietor grilled him about being underage. Burl told him his dad was supposed to drive down from Pharaoh to meet him at the

<166>

bus, but he couldn't get out on account of the storm. The man gave him a room. "But stay outa the bar," he said. As Burl could see, the bar was already full of grown men who couldn't find their way home.

He didn't sleep much. A country-and-western band played well into the wee hours. So he lay on his bed thinking through the plans he had made on the bus, turning them over and over in his jangled brain like a chicken on a spit over a slow fire.

Reggie had insisted on giving him some money. When it finally occurred to her, there hadn't been time to get to a bank machine, but she had almost eighty dollars in her purse. He didn't want to take it but didn't know how to stop her. Now it looked like it might come in handy. He had shopping to do in the morning before he caught the train, essentials for his trip up to Mile 29. There were things he needed that he couldn't possibly afford but could lay his hands on, if he was willing to make a little side trip before going up to Ghost Lake. A little side trip to Pharaoh. That was the catch. He didn't like the idea, not one bit, but the more he thought about it, the more he needed those things.

At Pharaoh he could get his snowshoes, his sleeping bag, some warm clothes, a kerosene lamp, an ax, and his Woods Number One Special pack, which was the only way he would be able to carry in all the provisions he needed even to stay just one night in an unheated cabin. The Woods Number One Special was big enough to carry the front quarter of a moose.

There was something else Burl wanted for Ghost Lake. A rifle. If he was to ever live there, he would need that.

The Budd left Sudbury and passed through Presqueville and then Pharaoh before heading northwest. It only went north every other day, so he'd be stuck in Pharaoh for forty-eight hours. He didn't plan on staying there. There was a hotel in

<167>

Presqueville. It wasn't much—mostly just a drinking place with a couple of rooms upstairs—but it would do. He could hitchhike down to Presqueville once he'd got his stuff from the house and hide out there until the train went north the following day.

If his old man still had his job, then going to the house would be a cinch. He wasn't sure what to do about Doloris.

The next morning, despite little sleep, Burl was up early. The storm had blown itself out, but the snow was knee-high. He bought a little single-burner propane stove, one cylinder of propane, and a can of kerosene for the lamp. There wasn't time to mess around with the faulty generator. Not this trip. He would only be staying in the cabin for twenty-four hours— the train south would come the following day.

He bought some groceries before leaving Sudbury—simple stuff, cans. There was a grocery store in Presqueville, but he couldn't be sure he'd get there from Pharaoh before closing time.

With the roads and sidewalks clogged, he just made it to the train. Out of breath, he plumped down in his seat. He was only wearing shoes, and they were soaked clear through, and his pants were wet up to the knee. He surveyed his purchases. It seemed so little. The whole time at Intervalle planning his glorious return to Ghost Lake, he had built up a stockpile in his mind. He had to keep reminding himself that this was only his first trip back and it had but one purpose, *The Revelation*. Reggie hadn't said so, but Burl was quite sure that if he failed this quest, he could kiss his dream place good-bye.

<168>

Back to Pharaoh

HE TRIED TO IMAGINE the conversation, how to explain what he'd been up to.

Would she give him a hand with the packing, or treat him like a visitor? Would she throw stuff, or would she be too drugged up to care? It's my stuff, he would argue. All I want is what's mine.

The car was gone. The path was snow-covered, with one set of big boot prints going out.

The radio was on loud. Country music. He paused on the step, shivering. She was singing along. He knocked.

At first he didn't recognize the woman who answered the door. He saw only that it wasn't his mother. She was short and busty in red jeans and a black sweatshirt. The sweatshirt read LAS VEGAS, HERE I COME! She had brown hair piled up

<169>

every which way. A cigarette hung out of her pointy little face. Same brand as Cal's.

It was Tanya. The girl from the diner.

At first he wondered what she was doing visiting Doloris, but then the room behind her swam into focus, and he grasped the fact that it was different somehow. It was tidier or something. Things were shifted around. There were a couple of new chairs.

"You're his kid," she said.

Burl didn't answer. He stepped inside, looked around. There was no chair by the window. Doloris's old chair was gone.

"Where's my mother?"

Tanya had stepped back when he entered. He was taller than she was. She looked confused.

"Whaddaya mean?" she said.

Burl's eyes searched the room. He called out. "Mom?"

"She isn't here," said Tanya. She turned to face Burl again and took a deep drag on her cigarette. "Whaddaya want? You can't just bust in here."

He walked through the room, looking at things, picking things up.

"Does Cal know you're here?" she said.

"No," said Burl, turning on her. "Does he know *you're* here?"

She laughed and punched out her cigarette in an ashtray shaped like a purple poodle. " 'Course," she said. "Cal and me are—"

Burl cut her off. "I'm not blind. Just tell me where my mother is, okay?"

"Jeee-sus!" she said, stamping her little foot on the floor. "You are a mean little cusser, just like Cal said. What are you going on about? You know damn well where she is."

<170>

Burl punched the wall with his fist. He left a knuckle-shaped crescent in the pressboard. It frightened him. It was the kind of thing he'd seen Cal do. "Refresh my memory."

"She's at her mother's," said Tanya, her voice trailing away. "Up in Dryden. Which is where you're supposed to be." It was beginning to dawn on her that maybe this was not true. She looked scared suddenly. Burl stared hard at her.

"Well, you tell Cal I came to collect a few things to take back to Dryden with me," he said.

Tanya sat down at the table, crossed her legs. He turned to a drawer where there was usually a cache of disposable lighters. He was glad to see that some things hadn't changed. He took a couple, shoved them in his coat pocket.

"Hey!" she said.

"That's just the start," he said, holding up his finger warningly. If she liked Cal so much, then maybe she liked being treated rough. His anger was like a volcano inside him. The punch had only opened a crack to let the steam out. There was no doubt in his mind, suddenly, whose child he was.

He opened the door that led from the kitchen to the woodshed. On a high, dirty shelf he found the kerosene lantern. Deeper in the shed he took a pair of snowshoes off nails on the wall. He tucked a crosscut saw and an ax under his arm. He piled these things on the kitchen table.

"What are you doin'!" Tanya yelled. "I just wiped that down."

She went to move the lamp, but he grabbed her wrist and held it tight. She got a frightened look in her eye. That calmed him down. He controlled his voice.

"I won't be here long. I'm collecting some things. Don't touch them. You can wipe everything down again when I'm gone."

< 1 7 1 >

She backed off. On the radio someone sang a hurtin' song. Tanya rubbed her wrist.

Burl headed down the hall that led to the two bedrooms. How low the ceiling seemed. He piled up some stuff on his bed, dug through his closet for his pack. He found a dirty sock encrusted in dust.

He stuffed his things in the backpack. He would fold them later; right now he just wanted out of there.

The master bedroom was all newly done up. There were flowered pillowcases and a pink comforter on the bed. There were pretty figurines along the windowsill.

"Get outa here!"

Tanya was at the door. She was carrying a long kitchen knife. "Just get the hell away from this room."

Burl looked at the knife, saw it shaking. He looked at Tanya's face. He looked around the room. It had been painted and dressed up so much that there was nothing left of his mother in here. He felt, for the first time, as if he was truly intruding.

"I only want one thing in here," he said quietly, not wanting to spook her, though he was pretty sure she wouldn't use the knife on him.

"What?"

"One of the rifles is mine. He keeps them in the closet."

"They ain't there." She nodded her head toward the hall. He followed her back to the kitchen.

"It was the first thing I moved when I got here," she said, opening the broom-closet door for him. She said it as if she couldn't understand how any woman would sleep in the same room as a bunch of guns.

There was only one rifle in the closet, way in the back

behind a new broom and mop. It was the old pump-action Remington .22 single-shot. It wouldn't be much good against bears. Burl had hoped for the .30-.30.

"He's got the others in the car," said Tanya. He dug a box of shells off the top shelf, carried them out to the table with the rifle.

Tanya followed him, but she had dropped her arm with the knife in it. He went on about his work.

It was strange. The house was slipping away on him. It was less his home now than it had been when he'd walked in half an hour earlier. Now with every passing minute, he felt more and more that he was the one who was trespassing. He would phone Granny Robichaud when he got a chance, to make sure his mother really was there. But it seemed likely. And as he thought about it, Burl couldn't figure why she hadn't gone years ago. There might even be a chance for her to kick the drugs up in Dryden, start a new life.

"You almost done?" Tanya asked. She had put her weapon away.

"Yes," he said. He packed his things carefully now. The woodstove was pumping out BTUs. Cal wouldn't like that. The house used a lot of wood anyway. Maybe he'd let her waste wood for a while—maybe he liked her a lot—but he'd crack down eventually. For a second, Burl actually felt sorry for Tanya.

"I thought you was with her," she said, maybe trying to make some kind of peace.

He didn't answer. Then he take-twoed it, cut her a little slack. "I'm sorry I was so angry. I was surprised, that's all."

"What do I tell him?" she said.

Now that they were more or less talking, he realized that

< 1 7 3 >

she was more his age than Cal's. He shrugged, not looking at her.

"Tell him I've found a really good thing," he said. "Make sure he knows things are going really well for me and that I wanted him to know that."

She clamped her mouth shut. He didn't think she'd say anything to Cal. Not unless she wanted a split lip.

A Windowless Night

IT WAS LATE in the afternoon by the time Burl reached Presqueville. He had walked almost halfway from Pharaoh before finally being picked up by a native guy in a pickup. He shared the bench seat with the whole family and a dog. The truck was badly in need of springs, but the cab was warm and the kids shared a bag of popcorn with him.

There was no room for Burl at the hotel. There was some major repair work being done on the line, and residence at the CPR barracks had overflowed into every available space in town.

He walked around with very little idea of what to do. Presqueville was long and skinny north and south, stretching along the railroad line. No crossroads went more than a couple of blocks east or west except for the main intersection, which was the road out to the Trans-Canada. There wasn't much of

<175>

a downtown. The Woolworth, a Safeway, the drugstore, a beer store at the end of a muddy side road, a couple of churches, the hotel, and a handful of other small businesses. In the Bide-A-Wee café Burl ordered some chips and gravy. He looked out the window into the gathering dark, looking for familiar faces.

At six o'clock Burl headed back down the main street toward the train station. He asked if he could leave his stuff there until the northbound train the day after tomorrow. Grudgingly, the attendant agreed. There were no lockers; Burl hauled his stuff out of the way into a corner of the office. Then he used the washroom, not sure when he'd see another, for the café had closed and he wasn't sure he wanted to risk going into the bar.

As he washed his hands, he read a sign for the benefit of the rail workers printed on the mirror above the sink.

YOU ARE LOOKING AT THE PERSON MOST RESPONSIBLE FOR YOUR SAFETY.

He had to smile at that.

The wind picked up, blowing the snow down Main Street and pushing him along like a piece of rubbish. He'd changed into some long johns he'd picked up at home. He'd also picked up his winter boots, but they felt a size too small now. He couldn't remember an October like this, so full of itself and acting like January.

Cal would be home by now. Would Tanya tell him about her afternoon visitor? Doloris and Burl had learned not to pass on bad news to Cal. But Tanya would have had some explaining to do. Cal would notice the .22 was gone. He had a nose for things of his that went missing.

The hotel was hopping, fatted up with extra workmen cold from a day on the line. Teenagers were hanging around on the street outside, waiting for a good fight, or something. Burl

<176>

was hanging around, too. That's when he saw the Turd-mobile. It glided by, decorated for a moment by the neon of a beer sign. Cal was alone in the car. He didn't see Burl. Burl pulled back into the shadows beside the hotel.

Cal was looking for him, and he had only himself to blame. "Tell him I've found a really good thing." It didn't do to be boastful around a man like Cal.

The temperature was dropping, and it was becoming increasingly obvious to Burl that he was going to be spending a night on the street again. But this was not Toronto. There were no all-night establishments to warm up in. What's more, it threatened to be a truly blustery night.

He headed down the alley to the back of the hotel. A dirt road ran between the backs of the stores on Main and the train line. Several trains stood dark and heavy, lit only by occasional beacons along the track. Hugging the shadows, Burl made his way south toward the train yards. Maybe he could find an open boxcar.

The road he was on ended at a chain-link fence. The schoolyard. His old school. He had stood at this fence watching the trains go by.

Laura had once come over to him standing by this fence, just about here. It must have been when he was just starting school. She was already in grade four. She and a friend of hers brought over her friend's little brother, who was crying. "Burl'll look after him," Laura said. She winked at him. He couldn't remember the friend or the little brother. He didn't remember whether he looked after the kid or not. Maybe they watched the tracks together until the bell. He clenched the chain-link. It had been right here.

He followed the fence around to where there was a gateway and then picked his way through the playground to the gym.

<177>

He tested the doors. Locked. But there were lots of doors in a school, and there were windows.

He was at the west end of the building, squatting in a basement-window well, when he heard the train coming. The whole squat body of the school stood between him and the gathering noise, but the window he was trying trembled in its casement as the train approached, a freight train with maybe a hundred cars.

In a flash he knew what to do. He slipped out of the well, found a rock, and beetled back. The train was thundering by now. Burl smashed the glass. He smashed away at it all along the frame until there wasn't a single jagged piece sticking out. He was in the school before the train had passed. He found himself in a sweltering-hot boiler room. It felt like heaven. At the doorway, leaning against the brick wall, he listened. There were a hundred sounds, but none of them, when he listened long enough, seemed human.

Burl searched until he found a room off the gym where mats were piled. He slipped in and pulled the door behind him. In a corner he rolled himself in a mat and lay there. If anyone came, he was trapped, cornered. The room was windowless. But as his heart slowed down to something like a normal rate, he came to the conclusion that being caught in here was not so bad. One thing for sure—Cal, roaming the streets in the Turd-mobile, wasn't likely to come anywhere near the school.

< 1 7 8 >

No Strings

NATALIE HAD CALLED girls' basketball practice for eight in the morning. It was a recipe for disaster, a gaggle of gangly twelve- and thirteen-year-olds, half-awake and tripping over their shoelaces. But no matter how fumble-fingered they were at that early hour, it had seemed better to her than after school, by which time the more mature among them would have fully remembered that all they cared about in the world was boys. Anyway, eight A.M. had seemed a fine time back in early September, when the sun could still be counted on to have made it up by then. On this dark, freezing morning in October, with snow swirling about outside, all Natalie could think of was that she was glad the tournament was soon.

The scream woke everybody. Two girls had gone to get the balls from the storage room. Now they stood at the doorway, immobile with fright but not at all subdued vocally.

<179>

"All right, all right," said Natalie, her voice echoing in the gym. She expected a mouse. She didn't expect a boy.

Natalie was not a woman who prayed, but she would later say of that morning—because it was the easiest way to put it—that finding Burl Crow was like the answer to a prayer. That he was cowering in a corner of the storage room only suggested to her that Providence had one heck of a sense of humor.

The girls at the door had scared him out of his bedroll. By the time Natalie arrived, he was peering out from behind the horse, his face still heavy with sleep, but his eyes thoroughly unzipped.

Natalie shooed her girls away and, having flipped on the lights, closed the door behind her.

"Burl?" she said. "Burl Crow. I've been looking everywhere for you."

David Agnew came by the school. He didn't have an appointment until later that morning. He took Burl back to their home. It was on a road that curved up into the hills just west of town. It was a log house they had built themselves on land they had cleared themselves. David showed Burl to a guest room in the finished basement. He flicked on a space heater. There was a bathroom there with a shower, if he wanted one. David apologized for not having time to make him breakfast, but he showed him where everything was. Then he stoked up the wood fire upstairs and left.

Burl was still only half-awake. The other half of him was afraid that it was all a ridiculous dream brought on by too many nights without a decent sleep. He fried himself two eggs, toasted some toast. Then he showered for about six years, leaning his cheek against the stall and letting the stabbing heat

<180>

dig out the hard knots of fatigue, which like pebbles and roots had buried themselves under the dirt on his miserable carcass.

Natalie was coming back at lunch, though she couldn't stay. So he thought he would rest until then. David had thrown a pair of clean pajamas onto the pillow in the basement room. Burl had never owned a pair of pajamas. They felt good. And the sheets were flannel and felt good, too, once he'd shivered the cold out of them.

Burl awoke and lay in the bed. There were comforting sounds upstairs: a radio, Natalie and David talking, kitchen sounds of food preparation, cupboards opening and closing, footsteps across the floor. Burl was amazed that they went to such trouble for lunch. It was only then that he looked at the clock radio by his bed and found that it was six P.M. He sat up. His clothes were folded at the end of his bed. Freshly laundered.

"Ah, well," said David, when Burl appeared at the kitchen doorway. "So there is life after death!"

Burl stepped sheepishly into the room. Natalie smiled at him as if he had just scored a hundred on a test. She dried her hands on a tea towel, came over, and put her arms around him.

"Welcome," she said.

It was that and the smell of spaghetti sauce bubbling on the stove that almost broke Burl. Like a car's windshield hit by a stone, he felt shattered into a million little round-edged bits at her feet. He held on to her tight for just a second, then let go and put his renewed energy into holding himself together.

Over dinner he talked, if it could be called that. It was more like when you kicked the branches out of a beaver dam, and the stream rushed through, soaking your shoes and threatening to carry you away. He told them where he'd been, where he was going. He didn't hide anything, didn't lie once.

< 1 8 1 >

"What happens next?" Natalie asked, when his story was mostly up-to-date.

"Next?"

"You deliver this music to Reggie Corngold in Toronto and then what?"

Then what. Then they give me the camp at Ghost Lake and I live happily ever after, thought Burl, but it sounded like a fairy tale.

"Didn't mean to pry," said Natalie, when the silence grew too large not to notice.

"You did so," said David.

"Did not."

"Did."

Then Natalie threw her napkin at her husband and he threw it back, along with a strawberry that was left on his dessert plate.

"See that?" said Natalie to Burl. "I'm a battered wife." Then her cheery face suddenly twisted. "Guess that isn't funny, is it."

"Yes, it is," said Burl, thinking of the strawberry hitting her in the shoulder.

"I'm sorry," said Natalie, suddenly deflated.

"About what?"

"Making fun of something as serious as that. I wasn't thinking."

David leaned toward him. "Nat made a little visit to your place. Had a run-in with your dad."

"Oh," said Burl. His face became grave. "What happened?"

"She drove over his foot," said David.

"I did not!"

"Did so."

Burl watched this verbal battle shyly.

"It's okay," he said. "I mean, about Cal's foot. He has a bunch of extras."

His hosts looked surprised. David started laughing first. Then Natalie. Then Burl.

"Does he keep them in a footlocker?" asked David. They laughed a fair bit more, and the sound warmed Burl and fed him like an extra helping of supper.

Then Natalie asked, trying to keep her voice light, "Where will you go?"

"Not back to Cal," said Burl.

"Good thinking," said David. "Best to leave him footloose and fancy-free."

Natalie begged David to stop with the jokes. Secretly, Burl hoped he would go on and on. But Natalie wanted answers.

"What about your mother?" she said. "Do you think she really is in Dryden?"

Burl shrugged. "If she is, that's probably the best place for her. Granny Robichaud will look after her." He imagined his grandmother and Doloris both clicking rosary beads together, saying their little prayers. Over and over.

David started clearing the dishes. "So," he said, glancing at Natalie. "You could go up to Dryden or take up Bea on her offer and live up at the camp."

"What about school?" said Natalie.

Burl looked from one of them to the other. He hadn't got this far in any of his thinking. A quest didn't have a "then what" that you could explain to anyone. You just did it, and what happened next happened next.

"Now we really are prying," said Natalie. "Sorry."

Burl didn't want to think about his options. In this spacious, cheery kitchen, his belly full, he knew that it would be a while before he could realistically sort out Ghost Lake. It was no use imagining it would just fall into his lap. So he guessed he

<183>

would probably head up to Dryden, when he had the money, though he wasn't sure there would be room enough for him there. He was just going to say this when David interrupted him.

"The thing is—what Natalie was getting at before she started throwing things—is that you're welcome here."

Burl fingered up a mouthful of the sauce still left on his dessert plate.

"Why?" he asked.

David shrugged. "Nat needs someone to nag about homework."

"No, really," said Burl.

Natalie looked reflective. "It's a good question. I guess David's right. I just need someone to nag about homework."

Burl shook his head. "I don't understand."

"What's to understand?" said Natalie. "We're greedy people. We've got everything in the world we could possibly want, and we still want more."

"I don't know what to say," said Burl.

"We'd like you to stay," said Natalie. "No strings."

"Except school," said David over the sound of the water running. "And dishes," he added. "Think seriously about it. Come here and you'll be doing dishes one hundred and twenty-one days a year."

"Leave him be," said Natalie. Burl got up to help clear. His jaw was clamped shut. To say anything would have meant undoing the muscles in his face, which would have been, right then, like undoing the knot at the end of a balloon.

David drove him to the train station late the next morning. Natalie had already left for school. She'd packed him a lunch for the train and written a note on the brown bag: *Have a good trip.* It was in her best blackboard handwriting. It looked so perfect: the loop of the *g* so generous; the little dimple in the top of the *r* just so. He wondered how long it had taken her to learn to write like that.

He stood on the platform at Presqueville waiting for the northbound Budd car. There was no sun, but the temperature had warmed up. Snow was melting all around them into pond-sized puddles.

Burl was on the lookout for the Turd-mobile. David had been talkative, telling him about his work up at the Leather Belt, but now he was quiet. It was a good kind of quiet. There were no secrets hiding in it. No traps.

The train came chuffing up the track, the air vibrating all around it. David shook hands with Burl, formal all of a sudden.

"Let us know anyway," he said. "What happens, I mean." He held Burl's hand firmly. Burl had to look away, embarrassed by the consternation on the man's face. He wished he had something stupid to throw at him.

"Sure," he said.

Then they hoisted Burl's stuff up into the baggage compartment, and Burl climbed up the ladder with a hand from the man there.

"If you decide not to take us up on this," said David, "at least come around and wash the dishes, okay?" Burl laughed. He waved good-bye from the wide baggage doorway while the conductor took his ticket. He waved again from the window in the passenger car, but David was walking back to his car.

When the train started moving, he opened his lunch bag. There was an orange on top with a number written on it in pen. Seven digits. The Agnews' phone number, he guessed. Everything in the bag bore the same number.

Before he'd finished the Hershey bar, he had that number committed to memory.

<185>

The Secret Drawer

THE TRAIN PULLED INTO Pharaoh half an hour later. No one got on board, but the Budd waited while a long freight heading south passed by. Burl scanned the handful of pickups and cars parked here and there beside the track. He looked as far down the dirt road as he could, expecting at any moment to see the Turd-mobile sail out of the mists like a Viking ship. It never came.

Burl's trepidation was like a small hard rock in the pit of his stomach. He had left the cabin so quickly, Bea hurrying him up. Surely he had not checked everything. Surely the door was not secure enough to keep away that bear. He let his imagination go wild for a moment, imagining the cabin a zoo of creatures large and small: timber wolves feeding on the carcass of a dead moose; great horned owls on the crossbeams, their droppings turning the floor into a slippery mess; a chip-

<186>

munk party in the grand piano; Reggie's army of mice in the briefcase snug in the tangled mess of *The Revelation*.

Immortality—it was in his hands. He owed this to the Maestro. No mice were going to take it away from him.

With an effort he shook the vision from his head. He hugged himself tight. The brush along the track was clogged with snow. Burl began to think about the trek in. Thank God he'd picked up the snowshoes. The wind would not be so bad in the bush, he told himself.

He got to his feet three miles shy of Mile 29 and made his way to the baggage compartment, where a couple of railmen stood jawing and smoking with a couple of hunters.

"Almost there," said the conductor.

"Yes, sir," said Burl.

Then they were slowing down for what seemed an interminable time, the honker going again and again.

"Be back through at around seventeen hundred hours tomorrow," said the conductor, as Burl climbed down the ladder to the ground. "We may be a little late, eh, on account of the snow." He winked. Burl nodded. He was hoisting on his backpack.

"I'll be waiting," he said. He stepped back from the track as the train started moving out. He waved, and the big door slid shut.

Burl slipped into his snowshoes. It had been a while. The tips crossed and he fell down. There was snow on the siding but not enough to cushion the fall. As the train pulled out of sight around the next bend, Burl clambered to his feet, ready, at last, to go.

The steepest hill was the one that led up from the tracks. The hill where the licorice grew, though it was well covered now. Burl was pretty good on snowshoes, but a hill was always a struggle.

It was the second time he took a nosedive that he heard the laughter.

"Hee-haw! But you're a sorry sight."

Burl swung around on his backside. There at the base of the hill stood Cal.

"Lucky it's not open season on ass-wipes," said Cal.

He was cradling his Marlin .30-.30 loosely in one arm. He held his snowshoes in the other. His hands were gloveless. Gloves were for sissies, Cal liked to say. Burl curled his own hands into fists inside his wet mitts.

"So this is the way to your real good thing?" said Cal.

Burl didn't move. Didn't speak. He wondered if he was hallucinating.

"Guess you're just dumbstruck with happiness to see your old man," said Cal.

It was twenty-nine miles to Pharaoh. If Cal let him by, if night didn't fall too hard or too dark, he could make it back in a few hours. Better than leading Cal to Ghost Lake. He began to slither back down the hill.

"Where you goin', scat-for-brains? Changed your plans? Ahhh, just when I was thinkin' we could have a little father-son time together. Like the good ole days."

Burl stopped and turned to look at his father.

He was already halfway up the hill, climbing toward the path.

"No!" said Burl, heading back after him.

Cal laughed. "Well, well. This must be some kinda special place." He clambered easily up the incline on all fours. "What're the bets there's a trail here as clear as a friggin' highway?"

Huffing from the climb, Burl reached the top to find the old man already at the head of the trail, puffing on a cigarette.

"You wanna hear how I done this?" he said. "You wanna hear how smart your undereducated old spit and blood is?"

<188>

He took a long drag. Burl rearranged the weight on his back. He knew that what he had to do now was not get Cal mad. Not getting Cal mad meant treating him as if he were God.

"I can't believe I didn't see you," said Burl.

It was the right thing to say. Gave the man a chance to make himself a little bit taller, and make the boy just that much smaller.

"I show up at the station in P'ville," he said. "I say, 'Pardon me, my good man, but I gotta buy a ticket for me and my boy. I'm meeting him here, but I got the funny feelin' he mighta already made the purchase in advance.' Sure enough. Return ticket to Metagama. 'Smart boy,' says I, and buys myself a ticket.

"Tanya drops me off good and early this morning down at P'ville and I make myself scarce. Build myself a little blind and sit waiting for the ducks to light."

Cal raised his rifle as if it were a shotgun. "Boom!" He picked off an imaginary bird and watched it fall.

"So who drives up in a Jap-fancy 'mobile—a car I seen before. And who gets all smoochy with some longhair?"

Burl just shrugged. To his surprise, he found he was listening to Cal in a new way. He heard how the man had to put everything down. Not only Burl, but everyone. Natalie and David—anyone who crossed his path.

His father tossed his cigarette in the snow, dropped his snowshoes, and climbed into them.

"Lead the way," he said. "I wanna keep ya where I can see ya."

He went on with his tale of how he'd got on at the very front passenger entrance of the train while Burl was climbing on at the tail end, still yakking with longhair.

Burl found himself wondering what his father expected lay

<189>

up ahead. He began to brace himself for Cal's disappointment when he saw there was nothing there for him. He found himself bracing for what might be a rough twenty-four hours.

The path was good, good enough that it had become a highway for deer and their pursuers. The leafless aspens trembled, branches clicking. Blue jays screamed.

"You find yourself a gold mine, boy?" Cal asked.

Burl shook his head. "It's just a camp. Nothing special. You're wasting your time."

The old man caught him up and grabbed him by the collar of his jacket. "We'll see who's wasting whose time."

Burl flinched but held his tongue.

"Hey," said Cal. "How can you *say* it ain't special when we're together again?"

Finally they came to the spot where the path led gently down into the clearing by the lake.

"Hee-haw," said Cal, evidently pleased. "A pyramid. We made it all the way to the friggin' Nile."

Burl was lost to hearing, lost in the sight before him. He had feared the cabin would not be there. That it would have dissolved like sugar. That his time there had never happened at all.

"This here's one helluva site," said Cal. "Um, um."

Cal stepped out of his snowshoes and walked across the deck while Burl dug the key out of its cubbyhole under the threshold. He didn't try to keep it a secret from Cal. He imagined Cal could smell a key as quick as he could smell live game. Cal took in the expanse of frozen lake with an experienced eye.

"There's good bass fishing in there," said Burl. He wasn't quite sure why—maybe just to tell the old man something he didn't know. Cal nodded without turning. The wind kicked his thick hair around.

<190>

The door was still in place. There were no bear marks. Burl unlocked it and stepped into the fusty darkness. He listened for the scurrying of creatures but was greeted with no sound at all beyond the creaking of a house settling into the wind.

He felt his father behind him, felt his breath on the back of his neck. Then Cal saw the piano.

"What the jeezly hell!"

He slipped a hunting knife from a sheath on his belt and cut the fishing line that held the blankets in place. With an effort, Burl kept his mouth shut. He took off his pack and stepped back outside. His plan was to take one of the shutters down to let some moonlight or starlight into the closed-up building, but leave the others up for extra insulation. As he pounded at the frozen fasteners, he heard his father hit a note on the piano. *Ding*. The sound filled Burl with fear. Then his father swore loudly, came to the door.

"There's no friggin' woodstove!" His astonishment almost made Burl laugh. "Who the hell would build a camp with no friggin' woodstove?"

Burl wasn't about to try to explain. "It isn't finished yet," he said.

"Ha!" said Cal, his hands on his hips. By now he'd checked out the electric stove.

"It's run by a generator," said Burl. "But it's acting up."

Cal kicked the cabinet. "There's no heat at all. What kind of a camp is this? Don't tell me—the kind of camp a goddamned longhair and his nosy teacher-lady wife would build."

He wandered around in the gloom of the failing light, kicking at things. He was obviously disappointed. Burl lit the kerosene lamp with one eye on his father as he neared the spot where the bulging briefcase leaned against the leg of the card table. He watched Cal's toe nudge it, then shove it a little until it fell over on the floor, as if it were a small animal he'd

< 1 9 1 >

shot but wasn't sure was dead. He bent down to examine the kill.

"It's just a bunch of papers," said Burl.

His father, squatting now, turned slowly at the hips and stared at his son. A smile started to crack on his face. He tapped the cold leather. "This the little gold mine, is it?"

Burl could have kicked himself, but he knew enough to turn away and busy himself with something else. He set up his tiny propane stove on the counter, stealing glances over his shoulder at his father rifling through the briefcase. After a good hard probing, as if there might be something of real value under the stack of paper, he gave up and left the briefcase where it was. Burl breathed a sigh of relief. Too soon.

"Hee-haw. What's this?"

Burl turned. His father had laid aside the briefcase. He was feeling the edge of the writing table with his hand. He bent down on one knee and looked under it. Burl watched with fascination. Cal pulled, and a drawer opened. A very thin drawer Burl had not known was there, had not noticed in a month of being alone in the cabin. From out of the drawer Cal drew some stationery, envelopes. He dug deep into the corners, still hoping for valuables. His hand came upon nothing more than an expensive-looking fountain pen, which he pocketed. He looked without interest at the stationery and threw it on top of the table as he stood up again, bumping the secret drawer closed with his hip. He glared as he passed Burl on his way to the door. He stood on the edge of the deck and had a piss.

Burl dug out a can of Irish stew from his backpack and opened it.

Cal sauntered back in, doing up his fly, and closed the door behind him. He picked up the can and poked the top off, took a sniff.

<192>

"You call this food?" he said.

"I wasn't expecting company," said Burl. He put the can on the burner while Cal stalked around the cabin like a caged animal. He fingered the piano again, the same note he'd played before. *Ding, ding, ding.*

Burl would not have thought it possible that anyone could touch that instrument and make it sound so unmusical. The note stopped abruptly. Cal closed the lid.

"So this is where it ended up, eh?"

He looked at Burl. He must have finally recalled that day down by the Skat last spring. It was strange for Burl to realize he had shared that moment with anyone else. He could see his father's face growing dark, as if the one memory had led to another. Burl wondered if it would occur to Cal that he still owed Burl a beating. Instead, he grabbed up his jacket.

"I'm goin' out," he said. He grabbed his rifle as he left. He came back a moment later and took the .22 as well. Burl wondered why he'd done that. Did he think Burl might shoot him? As his stew began to bubble in the can, Burl wondered for a moment whether he could do a thing like that.

But as soon as his father's footsteps carried him off the deck, his mind returned to the secret drawer. He raced to the table. The stationery was creamy colored and thick. It was embossed with the Maestro's initials. He had started writing a letter. The date was late in August.

Dearest Regina,

Yes, your real name, despicable as you may find it. It's a good name. Strong and regal. And nicely formal, which seems appropriate, since it's been so long since we last saw each other. Too long.

I've run off into the woods, Regina. I've found a sanctuary. No, I'm not becoming a nun, just writing. At last. I'm writing something quite grand. Don't worry, your lovely eyes shall be the first to see the fruits of my labors. It is nearly done.

But a remarkable thing has happened just this afternoon. A boy has stumbled out of the woods. I call him a wild child, but, in truth, he's an imaginative thing despite a harsh life full of beatings, unless my eyes deceive me. He is sleeping as I write this, lying on the floor under my piano. I feel very fatherly toward this urchin. And I feel, at the same time, completely

The letter went no further. Burl searched through the remaining pages. There was nothing. What had happened? A bear had scratched on the door. That's what.

Burl folded up the letter and put it in his pocket. Thinking of Reggie—Regina—he was reminded forcefully of what he was there for. Quickly he stuffed *The Revelation* in his pack. That was when he heard the gunshot. He ran over to the window. Nothing. He opened the door. His father was returning from way down the beach.

Cal didn't come into the cabin. Instead he cleared a place on the beach. He had found the ring of stones where Burl had made bonfires in the summer. Now Cal built his own fire. He came in finally, whistling to himself, and poked around until he found some salt and pepper.

"Enjoy your baby food," he said as he closed the door behind him.

Burl watched him from the door, even though it meant letting cold air into the cabin. The hunter rigged up a spit supported by crossed sticks. There looked to be a bird on it, though Burl had not seen him pluck and clean it. There was no denying the man was remarkable.

Cal showed no indication of coming indoors. Just as Burl was about to shut the door, he watched his father dig into an inner pocket of his coat and come out with his flask. He took a long pull at its neck.

Burl sat cross-legged on the rug near the one unblinded window, eating his stew. The sun was giving up early, heading home. Through the scudding clouds he caught a glimpse now and then of a halfhearted moon. Without his father in the room it was almost possible to recall the peace of mind he had known there. Almost.

<195>

The First Trumpet

AROUND EIGHT, Burl made a nest for himself on the mattress. He sat the kerosene lamp on the floor safely out of reach of the bedclothes. He wasn't sure if his father was coming in or not. He could hear him sometimes, snatches of whistling at his fire by the lake.

He wasn't sure what to expect. Cal seemed happier outside than inside, which was fine with Burl. He had no sleeping bag, as far as Burl could tell. He had only been carrying a small pack. But then his father was a man of many resources, and out in the woods he was in his element. If Cal did come into the cabin, he would expect the bed, in which case Burl would sleep on the floor, under the piano. It was only one night.

He got up again to pee. When he had finished, he went to the door and opened it just a crack. The wind was high, buffeting the cabin. It met him at the door hard in the face.

<196>

Cal's fire was now only glowing embers. He had stopped whistling. He was leaning against a boulder down low out of the wind's path, gazing into the low flames. He twitched and moved something from behind him, a stick, which he threw into the pit. He settled in again. If he had seen or heard the door open, he did not look Burl's way.

Burl closed the door and raced back to his blankets and sleeping bag, stopping only to turn up the kerosene lamp. He kept the can of kerosene and a flashlight nearby so that he could fill the lamp in the night if he woke up cold.

He had buried his pack with *The Revelation* in it under his mattress. He had stuffed the briefcase with scrap paper, hoping that his father would not bother to check it again or too closely.

He was beginning to nod off when he heard footsteps on the deck, and then the door opened. Cal strode into the cabin, closing the door behind him.

"You awake, boy?"

"What is it?"

Cal crossed the cabin in long weaving strides and bent down by the lamp to warm his hands over the glass chimney. He turned up the wick until the brightness hurt Burl's eyes.

"I just had me one damn clever idea," he said.

Burl felt cold air snake into the bed with him. It was coming off Cal, long snaky tendrils of draft. Cal sat himself down at the foot of the mattress. He chuckled drunkenly. He looked at Burl.

"You gonna be glad to see the last of me, ain't you."

It did not seem like bait meant to trap Burl, but the boy kept his face absolutely neutral, just in case. Cal, however, didn't seem to be looking for an answer. He rubbed his hands together. His face was glowing, heated by lamplight and by

<197>

whatever he'd been drinking. His hair stood up in ragged spikes.

"I'm prepared to cut you a deal, boy. I'm gonna give you your freedom from me, and all it'll cost is *that.*"

He pointed at the piano.

Burl sat upright. "What would you do with it?" he asked.

Cal rolled onto his knees and crawled over to the piano. He flipped up the cover. Still kneeling, looking back over his shoulder at Burl, his hands came down mightily on the keyboard, producing a horrible noise. Burl winced.

"Didn't know I could play, eh, Burl?" he yelled. "You any idea what this piece of furniture is worth in cold hard cash?"

"No," he said, though Bea had given him a fair idea.

"I'd guess quite a few thousand. Quite a goodly few."

This was crazy talk. Best to ignore it.

"Eh, Burl? Whaddaya think?"

Burl shrugged. He wanted to stay out of this, but Cal wasn't going to let him. He crawled back to the bedside on all fours and slammed his hand down on the floor. "I ast ya a question!"

Burl drew his knees up to his chest. "How could you get it out of here?" he said, as if his only concern were a practical one.

"The same way it came in," said Cal. He waved his arm around over his head in a drunken imitation of a helicopter.

"The helicopter cost a fortune," said Burl, unable to stop himself. "Anyway, how are you going to explain to them what you're doing taking it out?"

Cal's eyes narrowed. He poked his face toward the boy until Burl's head was up against the sloping wall. Burl turned away from the stink of the man's breath.

"You seem to know one helluva lot about it," he said.

Burl clammed up.

Cal began tugging off his boots. He stared at the piano. "I could drag it out of here," he said.

Burl lay down, rolled away, pulled the covers up under his chin.

"I could get a couple of pals with snowmobiles. Flip that sucker on its back like a dead moose and drag'er out." He started laughing. He laughed hard, slapping the mattress, leaning over to slap at the covers, where Burl lay curled up in a tight ball.

"Three of us oughta be able to do it. Flip that sucker over and just haul her outa here. No problemo. Hey, whaddaya think of that?"

Burl fought off his growing sense of alarm. There was no reason to take Cal seriously. It was just drunken talk. The idea was ridiculous.

Cal let out a great big roar of laughter, which ended in a coughing fit.

"Can you just imagine the boys down at the Budd when we show up with that piece of furniture—hey, fellahs, can you give me a hand? All aboard!"

Cal yucked it up for a few more minutes, then grew quiet. Burl listened closely. Quiet could be deadly. He dared to turn his head just enough to see what his father was up to now. Cal was between him and the lamp, and his shadow fell across Burl. Out of the shadow, Cal's eyes burned with their own bloodshot light.

"You don't seem to like my little brain wave?"

Burl cleared his throat. It was dry with fear.

"I thought you were serious," he said.

Suddenly, Cal was on him, his arms pressing down on either side of his head, his face pressing up close. "And what makes you think I ain't serious!" he said. He sat up again, sat on the edge of the bed, pulled off his other boot.

"You think I don't know who they are?" he growled. "That Agnew bitch, that nosy teacher and her longhair husband. Maybe these folks need a lesson, eh?"

"No."

"No? Did you say no?"

"I mean, it isn't their piano," said Burl. "This isn't their cabin."

Cal didn't say anything right away. He leaned back on his elbows on the mattress, looking around. He turned to Burl and gave him a dirty grin.

"So who else you been hittin' on, eh?"

Burl turned away again.

"Who else you tell your sob story to? Roll those big peepers. 'Please, I'm a poor lost boy.' You know what you are, Burl Crow? You're a slut, just like your mother."

Burl balled himself up in the fetal position. He lay like that, taut as a spring.

"Y' hear me?" said Cal. "A slut."

That's when the spring burst. Burl's foot lashed out, and even though it was swaddled in blankets and a sleeping bag, it made good contact. It caught Cal in the ribs just under his arm, heaving him off the edge of the mattress onto the floor.

For a moment Cal was too stunned to react. Burl landed another weak kick and a third, before Cal fended him off and managed to throw his body across the flailing legs.

"Little bastard," he roared, a big grin on his face, and he lunged at Burl's head. Burl slithered out of reach and fought his way out of the bedclothes. He tried to escape, but Cal tackled him, laughing now, as if it were just horseplay. With a snarl Burl pulled himself free of his father's grasp, and Cal was left holding only the sleeping bag.

"Why do you hate everyone!" Burl yelled.

Cal lunged again; his feet flew out and hit the kerosene

<200>

lamp. It teetered and fell and rolled toward where the roof met the floor. Burl danced out of Cal's way, the broken lamp tugging at his attention.

"Look!" Burl cried, but Cal didn't turn to look.

"You think I was born yesterday?" he said.

Burl dashed toward it. He could smell burning carpet. He could see smoke rising from the floor. Cal grabbed him in a bear hold.

"The lamp," Burl screamed, feeling his feet leave the floor. He kicked, and Cal growled in his ear. He wrestled Burl down on the bed.

"You crazy idiot!" Burl screamed.

There was a pause the length of a heartbeat, and then Cal's big fists rained down on Burl's hide like a rock slide.

"The lamp, the lamp," said Burl between blows. But Cal was lost in his rage. Burl couldn't see. There was blood in his eyes. "The lamp," he said, surprised at how far away his voice sounded. He struggled to get free.

Cal, oblivious to the danger, held him down. Suddenly Burl's arm was free from Cal's grip, and with all the power he could summon, he punched Cal, catching him hard on the ear. Roaring, Cal dragged himself up and Burl with him, lifting him off the floor, no longer hearing or seeing anything. He turned him around and around, and with a roar he hurled the boy as far as he could. He hurled him right off the end of the earth, past the moon, out of the galaxy, where Burl finally crashed into the Maestro's desk, which crumpled under him. Through the blur of his bloodied eye and the snowfall of swirling notepaper, Burl could see that the cabin was on fire.

"Slut!" screamed Cal.

"Watch out!" said Burl. Cal staggered backward right into a patch of new young flames as bright and bold as spring

<201>

flowers. He swore and stamped at the fire with his stocking feet.

Burl by now had climbed out of the wreck of the table. His body hurt, felt broken somewhere, but he had to get to the fire. Already it was climbing up one of the rafters. He charged at Cal, who was dancing around in his smoldering socks. He caught him square in the small of the back, pushing him back until he fell on the mattress. As Cal fell, his arm swept Burl down with him.

"Let me go!" Burl screamed. Again he wrestled free. Grabbing a pillow, he began to beat on the flames creeping across the floor. Cal came at him again, but lost his footing. Burl turned in time to see him stumble. He pushed him for all he was worth, sending Cal hurtling backward. Cal's feet were tied in knots of bedclothes. Rooted like a tree, he was felled. His big head hit the keyboard in a thundering chord. Then he crumpled to the floor.

Burl stood over him, breathing hard, frightened and fascinated by Cal's stillness. Then he started coughing. His eyes were stinging. The pillow in his hand was on fire.

He hurled it away. He turned and saw that the sheets of the bed were also in flames. Burl had no shoes on; he searched for something else to smother the flames—there was nothing. He grabbed at the end of the bedclothes, yanked them off the mattress. He thought of throwing them on the floor to smother the fire there, but it was beyond smothering now. So he hauled the burning load across the floor, gathering up the pillow as he passed it. It was like dragging a dragon by the tail. It resisted him, tangling in desk legs and piano legs, around his father's legs.

Finally he pulled it free and raced for the door. He dragged the dragon outside onto the deck and down the slippery stairs until he had pulled the whole burning mess beyond the reach

< 2 0 2 >

of the cabin, where he let it go. The wind soon whipped up the flames, and the sheets and blankets whirled in a freakish dance.

Moving out of the range of the smoke, Burl leaned against the deck, gasping for breath, his throat parched. He shoved a handful of wet snow into his face. Then he gathered as much snow as his arms could hold and ran back into the cabin. He had to get the pack.

His father had clambered back to his feet. He stood swaying, the can of kerosene in his hands. He was unscrewing the top. Before Burl's horrified gaze, he flung the contents of the can at the creeping orange carpet before him.

Drunk or stunned by his fall, Cal's reflexes were not sharp. He did not throw the can as well but let it dangle at his side. And the fire eagerly followed the trail of kerosene that led back to him. Before Cal could move, the fire was crawling up his pant leg.

Burl watched.

His father slapped and thrashed at the fire as if it were some annoying clinging child who would not leave him alone. He yelled at it and then he howled as it burned its way through his clothing to his skin.

Burl could not move. The snow, melting cold against his chest, seemed to stop his heart. He watched as his father fell to the floor, cursing and hollering, trying to unbuckle his belt, writhe out of this bright, new, scorching garment.

Then Burl's attention was diverted. The mattress under which he had hidden his pack was consumed in flames. He screamed and leaped toward it, only to be hurled back by a wall of fire.

It all happened so fast. He didn't recall making a decision. Cal had rolled over and over, trying to smother the flames. He ended up under the piano, which is where Burl had to

<203>

crawl to get him. He grabbed his arms and yanked. His father's pants were down around his knees, and Burl could see that the skin on the side of his thigh was melting. His father was unconscious, a dead weight.

Fire was falling now onto the shiny black top of the piano, burning holes in the lacquer, blistering it like the skin of some monster in a horror film.

Nothing could be saved. If Burl did not move quickly, not even he would be saved. For one horrible moment he didn't care. Then he stopped thinking and hooked his arms under his father's arms and dragged him toward the door. It slammed shut just as he reached it.

He panicked, couldn't move. In his mind he saw the Maestro frowning at him. "Now look what you've done!"

Then Cal moaned and the image evaporated, and Burl flung open the door and pulled the man to safety, his smoking feet thumping down the steps. He dragged him out across the snowy clearing to the beach. He left his father by the dead bonfire, leaning against the rock where he had been sitting so comfortably drunk and full only an hour before.

Looking back, Burl saw fire shoot through the roof, fireworks. As he watched, one whole side of the cabin sagged inward. He walked toward the blaze until he heard a huge piano chord boom out above the crackling of the blazing building. The sound echoed out and up into the sky and spiraled up to the stars. There followed a sound like a long train of firecrackers. The flames had found the box of cartridges, safely stored in his backpack.

< 2 0 4 >

New Shoes

It SEEMED ODD—indecent—that Burl would actually light a fire. But as the night closed in, a controlled fire became a necessity. It was too dangerous to stay near the burning cabin. The heat was too intense; the destruction unpredictable. And yet how absurd it would be to freeze to death a stone's throw from a burning building. So when his muscles had recovered sufficiently, and the ache in his side turned out not to be anything broken, Burl hauled himself up and with a long stick managed to drag a mat-sized chunk of the deck across the clearing and into the ring of stones he had placed on the beach in such a careful circle one fine summer's eve. The kind of fire pit his father had taught him to build. The wood was like a burning raft, sizzling along its prow as it plowed through the snow.

He went back for more wood, and the path along which

<205>

he dragged his burning supplies melted the snow and turned the frozen earth to mud, which oozed coldly between his toes. Cal, when he had come back into the cabin stupid drunk, had forgotten his coat by the bonfire. Burl draped it over him. He was still unconscious. By firelight, Burl heaped snow on his father's burnt leg to stop the flesh from melting away completely. He felt like a small boy playing sand castles. But the snow on Cal's legs melted again and again as it drew out the heat that seemed to have traveled bone deep.

As his bonfire grew, Burl also discovered the ax he had brought, which his father had taken and left by the fire. His guns, of course, he had not left outside. Even in a stupor, Cal the hunter would never think to leave a firearm out in inclement weather.

Kicking at the black remnants of the bedclothes, Burl found that a fair-sized section of his sleeping bag had survived, although it was charred and soaked in places from lying in the snow. He stretched it out on a boulder to dry by the campfire. Then he wrapped it around his father's shoulders. He had made one last trip back to the cabin while the entranceway was still an entranceway. The Maestro had left a coat hanging on the door. It was smoky but otherwise unharmed.

He found the small pack his father had carried in from the track. In it he found a plastic bag, and in the bag were the shrink-wrap and Styrofoam packaging off a chicken bought at the Safeway in Presqueville. That explained what the mighty hunter had been cooking over the fire.

Burl curled himself up near the campfire, looking back at the cabin from time to time as some loud noise indicated the collapse of another rafter, another section of roof.

At one point the piano thundered again. He imagined that its legs had burned clear through and the great shapely torso

<206>

had fallen to the floor. He recalled a trip to an abattoir with his father to see about getting a moose butchered. He had watched a cattle beast being slaughtered: first stunned by a hammer blow to the skull, collapsing on its knees. It was like that. The sweet black angel that had crossed his path down by the Skat looking like an airlifted cow was now knackered. Destroyed.

At some point he noticed that his father was snoring—no longer comatose, but sleeping fitfully in his down-filled jacket. Burl wanted to throttle Cal awake, smash his big ugly head against the rock. He wanted to drag him back along the muddy path to the burning building and throw him on it. Give him a taste of hell. Get him used to the idea.

Granny Robichaud was a firm believer in hell. Burl didn't used to think much of it, but suddenly he felt quite certain that hell was what you made of things. He imagined Cal being let into heaven, no questions asked, all his sins left behind. How long would it take him to turn the place on its ear? How long would it be before he was plucking feathers from angels' wings just for the hell of it?

Well into the fullness of the night, somewhere around the time when the wolves own the woods, Burl fell into a dismal sleep. He gave up the dark pleasure of hating his father. He had no energy left for it.

The sun woke him. The sky was clear, the air soft. He breathed deeply, only to fill his lungs with rancid smoke. Both fires were out: the one before him, cold; the cabin still sizzling and smoking. A gray pall hung over it in the unmoving air.

His father was eyeing him coldly. Burl looked down at Cal's leg. It looked like an overdone Christmas turkey. His father followed his glance, grimaced at the sight of his useless limb. He tried to move, grunted in pain.

"You're gonna leave me here," he said.

Burl didn't answer.

The man stared steadily at him, and Burl saw through the pain of his injury something weird, a kind of triumphant look hidden in the back of his eyes. If Burl deserted him, his father would have won some stupid game. He would have proven once and for all Burl's worthlessness.

Burl tore his gaze away from the man, started poking at the dead fire. A few red embers got turned up in the exploration.

"Why would I want to leave you here?" he said. "The CPR people saw us get off together—well, at the same stop anyway. Once somebody finds your dead and rotting body, I'll get blamed for it. No thanks."

Cal laughed, but the effort disturbed his leg, and his face contorted in pain. He swore. Gingerly he tried to move into a more comfortable position.

Burl heaved himself up. Every joint in his body hurt. One of his legs had gone to sleep; his bare feet were black with ash. He would have to figure out some kind of footwear if he was going to get out to the train, with or without his father.

He walked along the muddy path, now hardened again. Came back with a few sticks of lumber that he tossed on the campfire.

"What makes the most sense is to go out and get the train people to radio for Search and Rescue."

His father looked up at him, haggard but with that crazy glint in his eye.

"Like I said, you're gonna leave me here."

"Maybe," said Burl. "And if I do you won't know for sure if I told anyone once I get out."

He left Cal with that thought.

"I won't be lying here!" Cal yelled after him. "Don't think I'll be lying here." It was meant to be a threat, but Burl was beyond threatening by this point. He had things to do.

< 2 0 8 >

His first thought was to see what there was around that he might be able to use. Shoes, for instance.

He was already shaking like a leaf by the time he made it to the shed. His feet stung with the cold, and he began to worry about frostbite. It took all his concentration to open the lock, slide open the door. But his memory had served him well, and he sat immediately on a pail and began to work. There was string, and scraps of the tough black plastic material that had been used as a moisture barrier in the construction of the cabin. There was rigid blue insulation stuffed in around the generator, and Burl broke off a couple of pieces, which he fashioned into soles with his pocketknife. He strapped his foot and the ragged blue sole together in plastic and then tied the string around and around. He stood up. They weren't much for flexibility, and he doubted they would be particularly warm, but they were shoes.

He thought about making a space for his father in the generator shed. He could drag him up there; then at least he'd have some shelter. Then he looked at the path up the hill that led to the miner's cabin. He saw nothing but trees decked out in Christmas-card snow. It would be a long haul up to the ridge, with Cal fighting him the whole way.

Take Cal to the miner's cabin? What was he thinking! Somehow Cal would find a way to destroy the neat-as-a-pin cabin. It had to remain a secret. Burl had to have somewhere that was not his father's. It didn't matter how small a place it was.

He made his way back down toward his father, his new shoes squeaking with every step. The blue jays and chickadees were chattering; the sun was rising. Snow was already melting from the evergreens. Out toward the center of the lake he could see a stretch of open water, black as ink.

< 2 0 9 >

"Hey," called Cal when he saw Burl emerge from the bush. "Give me a hand here."

"In a bit," said Burl.

"I gotta piss," said Cal.

"Go ahead."

Burl looked again at the black junk heap smoking in the cool sunlight. There was no door you could knock on now—not three times, not even once.

From Out of the Ruin

CAREFULLY BURL MADE his way into the smoking ruin. His makeshift boots proved slippery, but the floor—what there was left of it—was too hot in places for bare feet. So he tore up strips of old blanket sufficiently wet from snow and bound his feet in them. There was shattered glass everywhere. He stepped carefully, testing each step for unsound wood; there was more of it than sound. And more smoke. He pulled his T-shirt up over his nose.

He made several trips into the wreck, using a pine branch to prod and sweep through the ashes. He found the second can of Irish stew, the tin blackened and too hot to handle. He scooped it out of the cabin with a broken stick.

He could see leftover construction material in the crawl space below the cabin. There was something else down there, too—the grotesque corpse of the piano. The crash he had

< 2 I I >

heard the night before had carried the huge instrument clear through the floor. Now only the iron frame remained in a tangle of coiled-up wires. One of the crosspieces had snapped. In the mud lay a heap of keys, so charred that it was hard to distinguish the white ones from the black.

His father called to him from the campfire.

"You expect me to look after this fire while you play games?" he said.

Burl found three more cans of food, some cutlery. He found the spring remainder of the mattress and under it the buckles of his pack. The score was there, too. It was stacked in a neat brown pile held in place by filthy strips of charred canvas. The manuscript teased him. He could actually read the writing on the title page—*The Revelation*—but when he reached down to try to pick it up, it fell away to nothing in his hand.

His heart broke. He had tried so hard; what else could he have done? The Maestro had stood on this very spot and told him that perfection was nothing more nor less than getting the result you desire. There could be no perfection now. It was going to be hard enough to survive. But he could do it. And that was something. Immortality would have to wait.

With his stomach rumbling and the cans of food luring him away, Burl was about to give up his search when he saw a glint of something. His battered harmonica. It was too hot to touch. He launched it with his scooper out into the snow. When he recovered it and put it in his pocket, there was something else there. Gow's letter to Reggie. Regina.

Cal was in bad shape. His face was pale. His injured leg looked raw. There was some kind of viscous yellow pus dribbling down it.

"You gotta get me outa here," said Cal. There was no bluster left in him. "S and R comes here, they're gonna blame me for that stinkin' mess." His finger was shaking as he pointed at the ruin. He seemed old.

"Then they'll be right," said Burl. He was busying himself opening one of the cans with his pocketknife.

"So it's my fault," said Cal. "It's my fault that you go running off and find yourself all kinds of fancy friends."

Burl looked at him across the campfire, a quick glance. It was a lot easier to deal with Cal when he couldn't stroll over and give you a cuff. He didn't need to say anything.

"Yeah, you keep an eye on me," said Cal. "Leaving us like that. Leaving your mother. Broke her heart. You ever think about that?"

Burl spooned himself some warm stew from the can. It tasted good. He took a second mouthful.

"You want some?" he asked.

Cal spat into the fire.

Burl ate in silence. Irish stew. Ravioli. Hot evaporated milk.

"Gimme some of that," said Cal. He drank the Carnation down to the bottom and threw the can into the fire.

Burl was up again, ready to work. With his father yelling after him, he went to where he'd stockpiled the odds and ends from the fire. A sled. How was it to be done? He had found his raft pulled up under the deck. When he flipped it over, there was a rounded bottom of ice that made it move smoothly along the snow, but also made it way too heavy.

Burl sat on the deck under the noonday sun, trying not to panic. The snow was melting. He was glad for the warmer temperature, but without snow, there was no way he could get Cal back to the track.

The train wasn't due until five. He would have to give himself lots of time.

He looked over at his father. Cal had found himself a sharp stick and was stabbing at the ground again and again. Why had he no advice to offer, only insults? What would he do in Burl's place?

A vision jolted Burl out of his stupor. A hunting trip with his father. His dad had bagged a buck far from camp. No four-wheel could get to where they were. No problemo. Cal sat Burl on a rock out of the way. Watch, he said. He picked two trees—young poplars each the same thickness through. He took them down with his hatchet, limbed the branches off until he had two good long poles. He took some rope from his pack, and, crossing the poles two-thirds of the way along, he lashed them together. Then he lashed the deer to the wide end of the contraption. Next Cal harnessed himself in at the place where the two poles crossed, so that a pole was under each arm. A travois. The Indians of the Plains used them harnessed to dogs or horses.

"I ain't getting in that thing," his father said. He had to rouse himself from a pained and jittery slumber to say it. He was in bad shape. He was hot, and his leg looked dead as slag.

Burl waited until Cal had stopped struggling, then, without a word, lifted him again. The curses flowed, and his arms flailed, but Burl got him on the ladder. He'd dug it out from the debris under the cabin. He'd made Cal a kind of seat at one end. It wasn't comfortable, but at least the patient wasn't going to be dragged along the ground, either. It was a lot lighter than poplars, and there was a lot of spring in it. There wasn't much spring left in his old man.

At the other end, Burl fitted himself between two rungs and gathered up the rails under his arms. He had padded the rung the best he could. Now he pressed his chest into it and pulled. His father yowled at the sudden jerky movement.

The travois moved a pace or two. Burl stopped, breathing

< 2 1 4 >

heavily. He took a few more steps and stopped again. He went to look at his father.

Through his fever, Cal managed a smile. "Can't do it, can ya," he said.

Burl looked at where the feet of the ladder at the cargo end had gouged into the ground. He looked at his father.

"I can do it," he said.

It took him another half hour to make a wooden runner on which the feet of the ladder could sit. The runner had to be pliable enough that its tip could be curved upward and held in place with rope like the front end of a toboggan. Then Burl reharnessed himself and started to pull. Much smoother. Cal complained, but he soon stopped grousing. Every bit of his strength seemed to be used up just staying alive.

The way was hilly. A lot of up to begin with and more down toward the end. The up was sheer hard work. Burl took each hill one pull at a time. He pretended each hill was the last.

When they had gone what Burl felt sure had to be halfway, he allowed himself a long break. He had saved one can of food. It turned out to be mushroom soup. That was going to have been his lunch. A hot pot of soup sitting out on the deck. Instead he was in the middle of the woods and the soup was cold, and there was no milk or water to mix into it. Still, it was sustenance. Through lidded eyes Cal watched him drinking the contents of the can.

"You gonna offer me any of that?" he asked.

Burl shook his head and kept eating, sucking the lumpy condensed matter into his mouth. He was doing all the work now; he needed the calories. He wasn't going to waste his energy explaining that to Cal.

They reached the track before dark. Burl had been listening for the sound of a train coming. He figured that if he heard

< 2 1 5 >

it when he was still on the trail, he would leave his father and run to the track. He'd heard nothing. He had to hope it wasn't too late.

At the foot of the licorice hill he finally fell to his knees. His muscles felt like mushroom soup. He had spun out his strength to the finest filament, and now that snapped. There was nothing left. He had spent the last stretch counting each step. He had got to three hundred or so before he lost count and gave up. By then his father was going through some new stage of suffering, and he began to jerk violently, once so hard that he lifted himself clear off the aluminum travois.

Burl cursed at him as he lifted him back on. He wondered then, for the first time, whether Cal would lose more than a leg. It was hard to believe that a man as powerful as Cal could be brought so low, let alone be finished off.

The train was late. They'd said they might be late, but they'd come eventually. And if there was no southbound, then there would be a northbound tomorrow around noon.

Burl tried to imagine making it through the night camped here in the open by the track. He couldn't make a shelter now; he was too weak, and he had left the ax back at the camp. But when the train still didn't come, he became sure that this would be his fate, so he ransacked his father's pockets for matches. There were none. How could there be so much fire one night and no means for making one the next!

Any minute. Any minute the train would come. He said this to Cal. By then he didn't think that Cal could even hear him. He didn't move from his father's side. Cal was as hot as a furnace, burning up with fever. He was rotting away. But while he was churning out heat, Burl huddled in close to the man.

He felt Cal steal an arm around him, though it had no strength to either hold him or do him any harm.

"You've got to know something," he said.

"Shhh," said Burl.

"I di'n' kill Laura."

Burl wasn't sure he had heard him right. "Shut up," he said.

"Your mother always blamed me. Always. I di'n' kill her. I di'n'."

Burl started trembling. He had been eight. Laura had been eleven, and then she wasn't. There had been weeping around the house and a burial. His father and mother had fought. Was it only then that the fighting started? Surely not. Surely they had always fought.

"Doloris said I shouldna took her with me. But I had to keep her with me. She was gonna leave. She was such a pretty little thing, and she was gonna leave us unless I kept her right where I could see her. I di'n' wan' her to go."

Burl looked into the darkness. Up ahead where the track curved, he saw a light turn red. That meant a train was coming from the north, though he couldn't hear a thing yet. He had to flag the train down. He tried to stand; Cal grabbed on to him.

"Doloris di'n' unersan'." His voice was disintegrating. "She though' I was just gonna show her off to the boys. Jeez! I'd a killed anyone who touched Laura. Doloris never believed me. Never."

Now it was coming. He could hear it through the rail first and then through the air. Finally he could hear the warning horn. He had to get up, wave the train down. It would rumble right past them.

"I'd have never let one of those guys at you, Laura!"

Burl struggled to get up. His father was holding him now with every ounce of his strength, as if Burl were leaving, too, as if Burl were Laura. Burl tugged at the big sweaty hand

<217>

attached to his shoulder. It was fixed there as though it were part of Burl, a heavy new appendage growing out of his shoulder.

"I've gotta flag the train," yelled Burl.

"She ran away from the party. How was I supposed to know she'd run away!"

"Let me go!" said Burl. He had stopped tugging at Cal's hand. He was hitting it now with his balled-up fist. But Cal kept talking, his voice all wavery like a station a long way off, coming in and out of reach.

The train was coming.

"She ran out from the card party, out onto the road. It wasn' my fault."

"Shut up!" screamed Burl in his father's face. He could see the headlight of the train now, lighting up the rail. His father was all over him now, sobbing horribly. And Burl was crying, too, crying at what he had to do. He lifted his arms high and brought his elbows down hard into his father's stomach. Cal doubled over, his grip loosened, and Burl wriggled free. He jumped to his feet and waved his arms for all he was worth.

"Laura," Cal screamed. "Come back!"

He was still talking like that when the crew hands jumped down out of the streaming light of the baggage compartment with their stretcher ready. "Laura, honey. I'm your daddy. . . ." They strapped him on and lifted him up and laid him down among the baggage, the skis, the mining gear, a caged dog.

Then the crewmen jumped back down onto the siding and picked up Burl, who had collapsed on his aluminum-ladder travois.

Japheth Starlight

GRANNY ROBICHAUD believed in God. Her God was a big grandfather with long snowy white hair and a flowing beard and stern eyes that could read your every thought just before you had it.

When Burl was at Granny Robichaud's, she always made him say his prayers. It wasn't something he'd kept up. But now, as his eyes opened, he began to pray—pray that this wasn't God sitting in front of him, inspecting him with such apparent concern.

His senses woke up one after the other. His eyes to God, then his ears to a murmuring hubbub all around him. The arrival lounge at Heaven Central? Burl blinked. God smiled.

"Looks like he's coming round," he said. Another face poked its way into Burl's consciousness. Not anyone with a halo or wings. A conductor in CPR blue, his tie askew and wearing

<219>

the same shirt he'd been wearing on the trip up, the collar badly frayed.

Someone else took a look, and then from somewhere in the hubbub a hand approached Burl, holding the top of a thermos filled with something steaming. Tomato soup.

Burl shinnied up higher in his seat and found that he was swaddled in blankets.

"Hey, hey, hey," said God, and clapped his hands together. Worker's hands, they were, with the ground-in stain that comes from sifting through dirt; the fingernails broken, bruised.

Around them, Burl caught a whiff of a rather ungodly aroma coming from the man directly across from him. Granny Robichaud's God didn't smoke a pipe, but this one did. Even as Burl took his first sip of heavenly soup, God settled back and lit up.

The conductor was not amused. "Japheth—jeez—can't you read the signs?"

Japheth tore his gaze away from Burl just long enough to answer the conductor. "Nope. Never did learn to read, Gabe. What do the sign say?"

A couple of other passengers chuckled. And then the conductor's radio coughed, and the engineer came on, speaking train talk. The conductor had to go, but not before he'd checked with Burl to see if there was anything he needed.

"Nothing," Burl tried to say. But no words came out. He cleared his throat. "Thanks," he managed.

"You want me to throw this old codger and his pipe out the window?"

Burl cranked up two or three muscles in his face and got out a bit of a smile. It didn't hurt too much.

This train was not bound for glory. It was the Budd car, worn and unlovely as ever.

The hubbub settled down and people moved back to their

seats. All except Japheth, who stayed put, smoking his pipe—
a white-stemmed pipe, as yellowed with age and handling as
the smoker himself. He kept an eye on Burl, but it was not
an intrusive eye.

The guy with the soup came back to see if Burl wanted any
more. Burl handed him the thermos cup and the man filled
it. Burl squeezed out another thank-you. His head felt thick
with cold. His torso and arms felt on fire where he had hugged
the ladder rails to his sides.

Finally, Japheth slipped his pipe into his jacket pocket. It
was a strange jacket, plaid, with big square lapels and toggle
buttons and a belt at the waist. It looked very old-fashioned.
Japheth combed at his beard with his fingers.

"You got on at Mile 29, son."

Burl nodded. Japheth looked interested. "I was a bit surprised
when Gabe told me. He phoned, see, when he got up to
Chapleau. That's where I'm stabled for the time being."
Japheth's hand would not sit still. It picked at loose threads.
"'A party coming out of Mile 29 today, Japheth,' says Gabe.
Thought I might like to know about it."

Burl stared at Japheth. The man's tongue was hunting down
some stray bit of tobacco. He located it, passed it to his lips,
and spit it out the side of his mouth.

"I got a little land up Mile 29 way," he said.

Burl moved, and the pain in his body seemed to flame up.
He grimaced. He looked down the aisle.

Japheth's brow furrowed. "You're probably wondering about
the fellah they hauled on board with ya?"

Burl managed a faint nod.

"He's up in freight. They're looking after him."

Burl relaxed a bit. It was as if someone had taken a heavy
bundle out of his hands.

"We haven't been formally introduced," said Japheth. "The

<221>

name is Starlight, Japheth Starlight. I own a claim, the north end of Ghost Lake. Perhaps you know the place."

Burl tried to swallow, couldn't. His right hand was buried in blankets. His fingers appeared from between the folds of swaddling clothes. Weakly he shook the prospector's hand.

"Burl," he said.

"It's deeded in my name, Burl. See, that's why Gabe was concerned about any comings and goings up there. Mind you, I guess we don't rightly own any part of the earth."

"There was a cabin there—"

"Up on the rise?"

"No, right on the bay."

Japheth smiled brightly. "So he got it built, did he, that piano-player fellah?"

"He got it built, yes...."

"And?"

Burl didn't want to go on.

Japheth's white eyebrows came together in a frown. "The fellah in freight," he said. "That looked like more than a campfire incident."

"The cabin burned down."

Japheth nodded. He seemed to have expected as much.

"I didn't know we were trespassing or anything," said Burl. "I mean, he was living there. The Maestro—Mr. Gow, I mean. I just thought ..."

Japheth was shaking his head. "He'll be upset."

"Who will?"

"Your—what'd you call him—Maestro. Mr. Gow. I do believe that was his name."

Burl pulled the blankets close around him. "He's dead."

Japheth looked up with surprise. "In the fire?"

"No, no," said Burl hurriedly. "In Toronto. The beginning of the month. You didn't know?"

Japheth shook his head. "Hardly knew the man. My, my." He scratched his head. "He seemed a nice enough soul."

Gabe came swaying up the car toward them. Burl fixed his eyes on the approaching conductor. Purgatory—that's what this was. Granny Robichaud had told him all about purgatory. It was a suburb of hell. A place where you are reminded minute by minute of every bad thing you've ever done.

Gabe crouched down, spoke quietly to Burl.

"We radioed ahead to Presqueville. They got a clinic there, but I suspect they'll be airlifting your friend direct to Sudbury General."

"That bad, eh?" said Japheth.

The conductor nodded. Then he cracked a bit of a smile. "He's ranting a fair bit. Seems to think he carried his boy out of the bush. Wants to know if he's okay."

Burl's face went stony still. He closed his eyes tight. This was purgatory, all right. Nothing good you ever did mattered. What was the use of trying? He opened his eyes at the sound of Japheth chuckling.

"That's a good one," said the old man. He looked at Burl, inviting him to join in the little joke. Then when Burl seemed not to understand, the old man reached forward and gently pulled back the blanket from Burl's shoulders. He was naked from the waist up. Japheth gently lifted his arm so that Burl could see the raw welts and bruises caused by the ladder rails.

Japheth winked at him. "Hard work being carried out, eh?"

Gabe pulled the blankets up around the boy's shoulders again. "Harder still carrying a kid out of the bush when you got no feet to speak of." He straightened up. "How far you bring him?"

Japheth piped up. "From Ghost Lake, Gabe. The boy dragged him out from the bay. Remember it?"

< 2 2 3 >

Gabe remembered. "What is it? A good mile and a half?" He looked impressed. "You done one helluva job."

"His name's Burl."

"Burl. One helluva job." Then he got businesslike again. Wanted to know who the authorities should contact. Burl told them about Tanya, how the only way you could reach her was through the diner in Pharaoh. She'd look after Cal, he told them. Then Gabe went off. For a few moments there was silence, just the rolling rhythm of the train and the sound of quiet talk, a little laughter, a friendly card game.

"I guess the authorities means the police," said Burl.

Japheth considered this. "I suppose. Injuries like that. There'll probably be some questions." His hands were clasped on his lap. He was not at all godly in stature. His feet hardly reached the floor. "If you went in there to make mischief, then as far as I'm concerned the cops should throw the book at you."

"It was an accident."

"Sounds good enough to me. Mind you, there may be insurance claims. I don't know what kind of thing Gow worked out. I just gave him the go-ahead. We didn't sign any papers or anything. He wanted some kinda tenant contract. If he was going to build this cabin, he wanted guarantees that he could stay there. I just had to laugh at that. 'What guarantee have any of us got,' I told him. I think he liked that."

Japheth smiled at the memory. "Still, he'd have been happier if we'd done business in a more businesslike manner. But I turned him down flat. He had my word that he was welcome there. Welcome to build himself a shelter. Come whenever he pleased. But nothing on paper. And I'm not sure if a company would insure a building when there was no signed agreement. That's just a guess, mind you."

Burl considered this matter as best he could. He tried to

imagine a criminal investigation, going to jail. If he had to, he would tell the authorities what had happened. But Japheth Starlight, now that he knew about the fire, seemed almost nonchalant about the whole thing.

"How did you and Gow meet?" said Burl.

Japheth dug out his pipe again. From the same pocket he produced a metal tool with which he reamed out the bowl, emptying the spent tobacco into the ashtray built into the arm of the seat. "I met him on a train," he said. "The Northland to Moosonee a few years back. He'd never been above the tree line. He was like a kid; he could hardly contain his glee. We had us some fine conversations."

Japheth, lost in memories, was tamping down a new wad of tobacco in his pipe. "I had a feeling he'd like it at Ghost Lake. I said to him, 'There, if anywhere, is a place a man could get his bearings.' You see, when I met him on the Northland, I thought, this is a man who needs to find his bearings. I told 'im that, too. Yessir."

"Well, he sure found it nice," said Burl.

"He did, did he?" Japheth was lighting his pipe now. He seemed to glow with pride.

"He loved it there," said Burl. "Being alone."

"Yes, he talked about that. Solitude. He talked about it the way a man who doesn't have much of it might talk. Me, I got solitude comin' out my ears."

Burl had to smile. Japheth seemed glad to see this. "Out my ears," he repeated. He started scratching at the straggly hair on his neck. There was something else on his mind.

"This fire. How bad was it?"

Burl took a deep breath. "The whole cabin. To the ground."

Japheth nodded as if maybe he'd seen a camp burn down in his day. "But it was just the cabin?"

"Yes," said Burl.

< 2 2 5 >

"No forest fire?"

"No, sir."

Japheth seemed relieved. "I have a modest little camp of my own," he said.

"Up on the rise," said Burl. "I saw it."

"How was it?"

"It was in apple-pie order," said Burl, happy to have something good to report.

"Apple-pie order." Japheth liked the sound of that. "Son, I've scratched and picked at just about every square acre of rock in this whole beloved province, and there ain't a nicer spot than that little piece of heaven. Not one. Not nowhere."

The train was blowing its horn like mad. Burl looked out the window to see where they were, but they were still speeding through nowhere. He had no idea how long it would be before they arrived in Presqueville.

Japheth cleared his throat. He was leaning forward, pipe in one hand, a box of matches in the other. He cocked an eyebrow at Burl.

"Let me tell you, Burl," said Japheth. "I find places you can dig up and pluck out a peck of gold or a truckload of copper or any of a number of valuable things like that old Mother Earth parked here and there in her great big bountiful body. But, you see, I also needed a place *not* to dig up, if you get my meaning. A place where nothing happened. So when I met your Mr. Gow on that Northland and saw the pickle he was in and the happiness he was capable of, I told him—go ahead, be my guest. Build yourself a tidy little place. Write yourself a symphony, paint a picture. Whatever. See, Burl, I wanted some artist there who'd mine some of that beauty, if you know what I mean."

Burl looked out the window at the bush draped in white,

lit by a fattening moon. What Japheth said had made him happy and then suddenly glum. "It looks pretty bad," he said.

Japheth had got his pipe going. He dropped his matches back in his pocket. "Well, that is too bad about the camp." He made it sound as if Burl had said they broke a window or two, scorched the counter.

"It's burnt to a crisp," said Burl, louder and more clearly.

Japheth nodded vigorously. He understood, but he seemed only marginally concerned. He frowned a bit as he worked through something.

The train thundered over a level crossing. The first they had come to. The highway up to Timmins. Outside the warning bells clanged, and the lights on the gates flashed, though there were no cars on this stretch of highway. It would not be long to Pharaoh. And then, another few minutes and they would be in Presqueville.

Japheth Starlight gazed out the window. Burl caught his eye in the reflection on the glass. He looked hard back at Burl's reflection, as though he were not a boy but a hunk of granite that might contain some valuable metal, and he was judging whether it was worth the effort to dig. Whether there was enough inside. "You're having some trouble with this, aren't ya?"

Now Burl felt sure he was going to cry again, like when he'd picked up the burnt title page of *The Revelation*. If he started, he wasn't sure he'd be able to stop.

"That place was the only time I was ever happy," he said. "Now it's wrecked."

"Nonsense," said Japheth. "This fire of yours mutilated a man's leg, and that's no joke. But he looks like a tough bugger. He'll pull through. And this fire of yours destroyed Mr. Gow's property, right? But he's dead."

Burl nodded disconsolately.

<227>

"So let me get this straight. The bush didn't catch on fire. And the lake didn't get burned up. Am I right?"

Burl frowned, as if he was being made fun of.

"Great," said Japheth, looking pleased. He was counting off on his fingers the things that had not happened. "And this fire of yours didn't burn a great big open pit, did it? No. So what was lost was something that had been taken in there. Nothing of the place itself was destroyed. Is that what you're telling me?"

"I guess so," said Burl.

"Well, then," said Japheth, leaning back in his chair. "What're you so upset about?"

Burl closed his eyes, too tired to argue.

"Oh, horseballs, kid. I'm not a fool. But let me rest your mind easy on something. Whatever the authorities have to say, Japheth Starlight isn't gonna grouse about it. I'm not much on material possessions. I like to know where my next meal is coming from. And I like a clean set of sheets to slide between once in a while after I've been out in the bush a long bit. I like a pipe and a beer with a friend and a tot of rye to warm up my innards when the north wind is having one of its bad days and wants everyone to know about it. I'm going to head on down to Sudbury tonight and have me a fine little holiday for a few days. Visit some friends.

"I think it's sad to see people crying over things. Now maybe you've lost something I don't know about. But I wouldn't cry about a camp. The place is still there."

It was then that Burl broke down. There had never been time. There had always been the next day to consider. There had been no room for grief in his life, though grief always seemed to be circling around just outside his door. He seemed to spend most of his energy keeping it at bay. He couldn't do that now.

< 2 2 8 >

He cried for Laura, gone so long. He cried for the Maestro. He cried for his father. He cried for his mother.

There was just too much of it all of a sudden. His barricades caved in. Grief kicked a hole in his carefully laid dam, and there was a lake's worth of tears ready to spill out.

At some point a handkerchief was thrust into his hand. He felt his blankets rearranged on his shoulders and a hand rubbing his back. He struggled to gain possession of himself.

The circle of faces was there again. The prospector. The soup man. Gabe, the conductor. Burl sniffed and wiped his nose, his eyes.

"A lot of people get like that when they talk to Japheth too long," said Gabe. The trio laughed a bit.

The train slowed down and pulled into Pharaoh. No one got off or on.

The train pulled out, and a few people started getting packed up to get out at Presqueville. Japheth sat quietly. The others had left.

"I'm sorry," said Burl when he caught the man's eye.

"For cryin'?"

"No. For what happened up at Ghost Lake."

"Well, now, I'd sure like it if the mess got cleaned up a bit. Nature'll do it, of course, but she'll take her own sweet time. But you could do it lickety-split once the summer comes."

"I can go back?"

Japheth hooted and tapped his pipe stem against the side of his head. "You are thickheaded, boy. Sure, you can go back. Anytime. In fact, you have to. I'm ordering you to. You've gotta clean up that mess back there. You made the mess— you clean it up. That's the way you become master of your own destiny, the way I see it.

"And who knows when I might decide to drop around," said Japheth. "Take a bit of a holiday in my apple-pie camp."

< 2 2 9 >

"I'll clean it up," said Burl.

"Good. Rake over the coals. Give old Mother Nature a bit of a hand."

The summer, thought Burl. As soon as it was warm. He would go again in the summer. And this time he had been invited.

He would write to Bea and tell her about the fate of the camp. If she was still interested in flying people there, she would have to contact the owner, Japheth Starlight of Chapleau. Burl owed her that much, he decided. He wondered if he would ask her for what she owed him. He decided he didn't want it, not now.

And Reggie? He would tell her what had happened. He'd send her the money she'd given him when he could. What else could he do? Would he send her the letter? He'd have to think about that. There was nothing left of *The Revelation*. Well, almost nothing. There were the few chords the Maestro had taught him, but the world would never get to hear Nathaniel Orlando Gow's oratorio. The Shadow had won in the end. If only the Maestro had found Ghost Lake earlier. If only Cal . . .

No. He wasn't going to waste his time thinking about what might have happened. He would clean up the mess. That was all he could do.

He would write to his mother. But he couldn't go up to Dryden, no more than he could move in with Cal and Tanya. He would plan to visit sometime. If she wanted him to.

There was nothing left to deal with but Cal. Cal and the memory he dragged around with him of Laura. But that was not a burden Burl could shoulder right now. Later, maybe.

"There she is," said Japheth Starlight. He was looking down the track to where the lights of Presqueville beamed like a few cold stars. "Is this your stop, Burl?"

<230>

A phone number flashed in Burl's head. A number he had seen written out in careful letters on an orange, a banana, the wrapper of a chocolate bar, a label stuck to a bag full of sandwiches, even scratched onto the top of a can of soda.

"Yes," he said. "This is my stop." And then he stood up on his shaky feet and put aside his blankets. The soup man hopped up and handed Burl his shirt and Gow's old coat from the storage rack above the seat and helped Burl into them. Burl shook his hand. He shook Japheth Starlight's hand. Then he headed down the car to make sure his father was looked after okay.

It was only then that Burl noticed that someone had found him a real pair of shoes. They seemed quite new, and they fit him well.

< 2 3 1 >